"I'm jealous of the air
that touches you, Erica."

She closed her eyes for a second at his seductive touch, savoring the sweet rush of heat in her limbs. This was Kyle again, not the stranger whose distant manner so frightened her. "Kyle..."

"No more talk," he whispered fiercely. "I know your loyalty, Erica. God, I never meant to drag you into this." His mouth suddenly claimed hers, with a searing pressure of urgency and hunger. "I need you as I need breath..."

"Kyle..." It wasn't his words so much as the desperate intensity she sensed behind them. Suddenly, it only made sense to reach out, to cleave to him, to try to bridge the distance between them at a level more basic than talk.

Jeanne Grant *is a native of Michigan, where she and her husband own a cherry, peach, and strawberry farm. In addition to raising two children, she has worked as a teacher, counselor, and personnel manager. Jeanne began writing at age ten. She's an avid reader as well, and says, "I don't think anything will ever beat a good love story."*

Dear Reader:

What better month than February, the most romantic time of year, to celebrate a TO HAVE AND TO HOLD mini-anniversary! We started publishing TO HAVE AND TO HOLD only five months ago, and already it's become a highly acclaimed romance line.

Your letters are providing some interesting insights into its success. Many of you were looking forward to TO HAVE AND TO HOLD because of its unique concept of married love, and we're delighted to hear that the books meet your expectations. Others of you wondered if stories of marriage would be as exciting and romantic as those of courtship, and we're equally pleased to hear that TO HAVE AND TO HOLD has convinced you they can be!

In both TO HAVE AND TO HOLD and SECOND CHANCE AT LOVE we strive to bring you the best in romantic fiction. It's our aim to make all our books of such consistently high quality that you'll be as eager to try our exciting new writers as you will be to follow your tried-and-true favorites.

We also work at giving you variety—the spice of life! Within each line we offer a range of approaches—from romances that will tug your heartstrings to those that will tickle your funny bone, from love stories that will set your pulse racing to those that will wrap you in gentle splendors . . .

When you finish our books each month, we hope you feel totally satisfied, as if you've just experienced the best of the many wonderful things love has to offer. So why not take a few minutes to jot down your thoughts about our books and authors and send them along to us. Your opinions are what guide us.

To all our readers, we wish you a most romantic Valentine's Day.

Warmest regards,

Ellen Edwards

Ellen Edwards
TO HAVE AND TO HOLD
The Berkley Publishing Group
200 Madison Avenue
New York, N.Y. 10016

To Have and to Hold

SUNBURST
JEANNE GRANT

A
SECOND CHANCE AT LOVE
BOOK

Second Chance at Love books by
Jeanne Grant

MAN FROM TENNESSEE	#49
A DARING PROPOSITION	#149
KISSES FROM HEAVEN	#167

To Have and to Hold books are published by
The Berkley Publishing Group
200 Madison Avenue, New York, NY 10016

1

DRESSED IN A threadbare T-shirt and paint-spattered cut-offs, Erica McCrery blew a strand of strawberry-blond hair from her eyes and rocked back on her heels to survey her project. The oak roll-top desk was an absolutely delicious prize, intricately scrolled and radiating four generations of character . . . but restoring it was giving her fits. A previous owner had covered the fine oak with a dark mahogany stain, which the customer wanted removed—a job that was not easy.

Finally, she had discovered the right stripping agent, and now she took up the cloth again, her concentration total. The day was still hot; the late afternoon May sun dappling a diamond pattern on the back of her kerchiefed head. Her long legs, coiled under her, were gradually beginning to ache from their cramped position. There was a splotch of stain on her turned-up nose and another on her chin, and her slim hands were covered with it.

"Erica? What's for dinner?"

"Ice water," she said absently. "Fresh-baked air and an extremely nutritious casserole of nothing . . ." She turned to the doorway with an impish grin for her husband.

Kyle chuckled. "You know I hate leftovers." Leaning against the doorway with one arm, he used the other to wipe a thin film of perspiration from his forehead. Then, hands on hips, he surveyed first Erica and then her project, with suddenly narrowed eyes. His smile abruptly faded. "What have you taken on now, lady?"

"Just a little desk. It won't take me long."

As he stalked forward, his eyebrows rose expressively at the discrepancy between her definition of little and the massive desk that had taken four men to bring in.

"It's a beauty, isn't it?" Erica insisted.

He nodded, but there was no answering smile, and while he studied her project, she studied him. After six months, Erica was still trying to get used to Kyle in a different working uniform. She used to think that nothing could accent his black-Irish good looks more than a suit and starched shirt. With thick black curly hair and a pair of flashing turquoise eyes, Kyle had projected drive and assurance in business attire, an aura of strength and controlled power tempered with a sense of humor. He had a more casual look now, in his dark, loose sweat shirt, jeans so worn and soft that they molded themselves to his muscular thighs and hips. But the soft texture of his clothes was denied by the new hardness she saw beneath the surface, from the lean, whipcord muscles that had developed with six months of physical work to the grimly determined expression that had replaced the old gleam of laughter in his eyes.

"Honey . . ." He rocked down on his heels next to her. "Oak's a bitch to restore, isn't it?"

She smiled again, radiantly, relieved there would be no argument. "Incredible. But the desk is so gorgeous! There are two secret drawers and a little hidden cubby-hole—"

"Erica."

She glanced back at him, only to find a white rag blocking her vision as he gently rubbed at the stain on her nose. His tender touch was a total denial of the harsh quality of his voice.

"You've taken on too much."

"I haven't," she denied.

"You have. We haven't had a decent dinner in three days; you're running exhausted every evening; and it would be different if I couldn't handle the business, Erica—but I know why you're doing it and it's completely unnecessary. If you want to do something, do what you did in Florida. You liked that historical society—"

"Kyle—"

"No more of it," he said flatly. He stood back up, hands on hips again.

She drew in her breath, frightened of that new glacier-blue in his eyes. "You've only got so many hours in a day, Kyle. You can't possibly do it all..." Instinctively, she stood up, too, but he stepped back before she could touch him, and rubbed his forehead with the tips of his fingers again. He was exhausted and fighting it. "Kyle, I like the work," she said softly. "Can't you understand—"

"I understand exactly," he said wearily. "Hell, Erica, I..." He shook his head as if he could shake off the bleakness that had come with too many overburdened days, and then gave up. "I've got to go out."

And then he was gone, with the chilling abruptness that was so typical of him these days. Erica automatically picked up the cloth again and dipped it in the solution, trying to convince herself that her whole body didn't suddenly feel tense and off-balance. She studied the wood she was working on, but the project had lost some of its fascination. A few minutes ago, the work had given something back... a beauty, a texture, a feeling of creativity and personal satisfaction, feelings she was only beginning to realize were intensely important to her.

Now she felt appallingly unsure, all too aware what an amateur she was. Half a year ago she would not have known the difference between oak and any other light wood. In itself, that was no crime. Nor was the liberal arts degree that had never been intended as anything but window dressing, nor were the social graces she'd learned rather than practical skills, or the fancy hors d'oeuvres she could still whip up faster than hamburgers. There wasn't anything wrong with the way she had been raised; it was all just so... *useless*. She felt an impatient, idiotic blur of moisture fill her eyes.

The mahogany coat on one drawer was very thick. Erica rubbed at it determinedly, but her own anxiety wasn't so easy to wipe away. It wasn't the bit of an argument, but that single instant when Kyle had pulled back from the touch of her. She was afraid...

Was she losing him?

Even the fleeting thought struck such an anguished chord inside her that she promptly blocked it, remembering instead how it had been when she'd first met Kyle. She'd thought herself so very confident around men, such an expert at saying a tactful no, that she was still a virgin; she was even rather amused at the chaotic, passionate involvements her friends took on. Then she'd met Kyle and was in bed with him almost before she'd memorized his last name; his pursuit had been so immediate and so potent and so total... There had been no cooling of his ardor in the last nine years, no time when he had ever been less than a virile and demandingly passionate lover. Only lately, since his father died...

He was tired, she reminded herself. Exhausted.

She stood up. The desk was done, a rich pale gold in the fading sunlight. It was getting too late to see by natural light anyway, and Erica was physically drained. Cramped muscles, tired eyes... and the scent of the stain, usually pleasant, was now strangely foreign, arguing with her empty stomach.

She stretched with a weary sigh, and half listened for Kyle's return as she moved through the shop to the little washroom beyond. She was cleaning her fingers in a small bowl of paint thinner when she heard the shop's back door open. "Kyle! I'm here!" she called out, hearing the slight lilt in her voice in spite of herself.

But it was not Kyle who found his way to the door. The man who entered was the diametric opposite of Kyle in appearance. His white shirt was still crisp over a husky though not heavy frame, and he wore the most expensive of suits, pearl gray, customed tailored. He had tossed the suit jacket over one shoulder and loosened his tie; his blond hair was a bit disheveled from the hot afternoon wind, and there was a lazy look in his brown eyes that she remembered well. He took one look at Erica and started laughing, approaching with the wariness of one who had to search to find a place to kiss. With both hands on her waist from behind, he nudged at the strands of her hair at the nape of her neck and kissed with a tickle.

"Morgan! You devil!" she scolded, her eyes automatically brightening at the sight of him. "We haven't seen you in so long!"

"I just can't believe it! Miss Country Club turned worker! Honey, when you strip down to the essentials . . . *lush*," he praised her appearance, examining with relish and in detail her long legs and feminine figure. "You get better looking every time I see you, Erica."

"Well, of course," she said cheekily, knowing exactly what she looked like next to Morgan Shane in his expensive attire. She was barefoot, her hair was tangled, and she wore no bra under a T-shirt that should have been in the rag bag. Still, he had the gift. When she first met him she'd been unnerved by the way he mentally undressed anyone in skirts, and because he'd been Kyle's closest friend he'd been difficult to avoid. Now she felt only a bubble of amusement at his survey of her, immediately aware that Morgan realized she wore no bra, and that her figure was more than passable. Her ego had been low and promptly climbed two notches. "But what are you doing here, Morgan? Aren't you a little far from palm-tree country?"

"Shane, Inc., decided to have a little look-see in the

Midwest with a view toward expansion. That was the excuse. The real reason was to find out why you and Kyle haven't surfaced above ground since you came to Wisconsin—and besides, I figured you'd be bored by now with no uninvited strangers dropping by once a month to mess up your plans."

"You're hardly a stranger. And you could have called ahead of time," she scolded. "It might just have occurred to you that I'd need thirty seconds to put the house in order and make up a bed."

"I brought dinner," Morgan said, defending himself. His eyes were flickering over the shop, and he didn't bother to hide his astonishment. "It actually looks as if the two of you are taking this hobby of yours seriously!"

"Hobby?" she asked blankly as she finished cleaning her hands, rubbed a small amount of cream on them, and reached promptly for the grocery bag he was more than patiently holding. She forgot about his strange characterization of their work as she rummaged within. "Steaks! You adorable man, you've brought a feast!"

And he brought the cooking skills to go with it. Morgan probably knew his way around a kitchen better than she did—cooking, she often teased him, was his second-favorite bachelor's hobby. She was duly shooed upstairs to shower and change while he marinated the steaks. Within a half-hour they were both seated in the living room. Morgan had uncorked the wine and was pouring it into two glasses.

The long cotton dress Erica wore was older than sin and intended for such. Once Kyle's favorite, it was a mix of forest and leaf greens, with a low smocked bodice and loose, flowing skirt. Barefoot still, with her hair streaming to her shoulders, she had a sensual sparkle in her eyes that the man across from her made no secret of appreciating.

Erica, on the other hand, was noting with amusement that Morgan had lost no time in making himself at home. His tie littered one table, and his coat was draped on

another; his shoes were already discarded by the couch
and his keys and reading glasses were stashed on the
bookshelves. When he left the next day, which she'd
already been informed was the plan, she would have to
trail after him the way a mother did a two-year-old. But
then, it had been exactly that way on his frequent and
just as impromptu visits in Florida.

"I still can't believe you're really living here," he
remarked. "I knew that when Kyle's father died you sold
up lock, stock, and barrel, but I thought you'd be out of
this little town by now."

"Mmm," she answered absently as she sipped the
smooth light wine. "You'd be surprised how easy it is
to get addicted to quiet and country, your work right
outside your back door, and your hours your own. Kyle's
family did woodworking for generations, you know . . ."
Speaking of her husband made her conscious of his absence, and she wondered uneasily where Kyle had gone.

"But it's hardly your style, love." He settled back
against the couch and surveyed the room, his gaze coming back to her with an affectionate smile.

The comment struck her as strange, and she stared at
him in puzzlement.

"Well, it isn't, honey," Morgan said dryly. "God knows
what's gotten into Kyle. In college, he used to swear
he'd never come back here; he hated everything about
the place. Manual labor? And for you—"

She shook her head at him. "I've never met such a
total snob in my entire life. Get off it, Morgan. You say
'manual labor' as if you'd have to get up and wash your
hands afterward," she teased. "And just for that, you've
got KP after dinner."

He chuckled. "I didn't mean—"

"You certainly did. I haven't the least idea what you're
trying to imply, but I am absolutely in love with this
place. Now that I've made it look so fantastic . . ." She
grinned impishly. "You should have seen it when we
first moved here."

It was not exactly fantastic, their little A-frame house. Their home in Florida, for instance, had been a breeze to decorate: She had merely walked into the best furniture store in town and hired the best decorator. Not this time, though. Erica hadn't known how long Kyle wanted to stay, and in addition to the shock of Joel McCrery's death, there was the shock of having to count pennies for the first time in her life. The transition from affluence to debt had been abrupt, mind-boggling; but the worst part of it had been Kyle's unwillingness to tell her anything. Still . . .

Her eyes skimmed over the changes they had made. A dark pumpkin-colored carpet covered the large living room floor. Cabinets took up one wall: bookcases, a stereo unit, and wood carvings. An imposing piece of driftwood served as the base of a coffee table, with a thick plate-glass top. Her huge crewelwork patterns in the oranges and creams and greens that she loved were centered above an oversized couch upholstered in olive. The living room was sunken; three steps up was the kitchen, with a low tan brick wall serving as a divider between the two areas. Copper pans and plants hung from the ceiling. It was all very bright and very simple, and Erica found more richness in the room than she had ever found in the luxurious surroundings she had been accustomed to from childhood on. "The place on the beach seems sterile now," she said musingly. "I'm not sure I'd ever want to go back."

"Sure," Morgan agreed dryly. "Have another drink, sweetheart."

He clearly didn't believe her. "Do you honestly dislike this house?" she insisted.

"It's a measure of your ability to make a home out of anything, Erica. I just have a hard time picturing the two of you in anything so small. Where is your weaker half, anyway?"

"Kyle? He'll be back any minute." She smiled obligingly at his quip, but was uncomfortable at not being able to come up with the exact wheres and whens for her husband. For no real reason, Morgan was the last person she would want to know there was trouble between herself and Kyle. "Tell me what's been going on since we last saw you," she urged.

Morgan hesitated, swirling the wine in his glass. "The business is going terrific, if you can believe that in these economic times. We've been checking out markets in Milwaukee, Chicago, any number of—"

"You know darn well I don't mean that," she chided. "What about Marissa?"

"My God, I haven't seen you in a long time," he said dryly as he took a long drink of the wine.

"So you've taken up the hunt again?" Erica shook her head, feeling a mixture of sympathy and exasperation with him. "I thought you were almost talking rings a few months ago."

Morgan shifted to a standing position and poured them both a second glass of wine. When he turned back to Erica, the teasing was gone from his eyes and he looked tired, the crow's-feet prominent at the corners of his eyes. "There's not much point in getting married when the chances of divorce are edging toward fifty percent, now, is there?" he asked idly. "My married friends aren't exactly advertisements for wedded bliss—you two are the only exception. At times I don't know what I'd do without the pair of you. Since you moved, I've felt as if my oasis has been ripped out from under me; your home was the only place I could go to get out of the rat race." He laughed shortly. "Sometimes I've wondered, Erica, if you offer everyone the chance to pour out their troubles to you, or is it just me?"

"Trouble, Morgan?" she asked gently. The brooding quality in his voice immediately aroused her maternal instinct. She had no doubt that across a board room Morgan was a solid and ruthless adversary, but when he came to stay with them he always had a stray-cat quality. His life was one long howl at night, with lonely silences in between. He always picked women who were takers, as he was, but Erica had the unaccountable notion that a single long stroke down his back would soothe the ruffled fur that seemed a by-product of his frantic lifestyle.

"I look at you and Kyle," he said frankly, "and I'm jealous. I've always been jealous. The way Kyle just picked up and moved, chucked everything on a whim. I wouldn't choose this lifestyle, but that's not the point. It's the inner freedom, the courage to just get out and do it. Change. Even if it's only short term."

Erica half-frowned. Neither freedom nor choice had motivated their move to Wisconsin. Nor were they engaged in a "hobby." It had never occurred to her before that Kyle hadn't told his closest friend the real circumstances following Joel's death. But before she could say anything, Morgan was rambling on. "I've been tied to the business ever since I got out of school, and there are times I'd just like to say to hell with it."

"Morgan," Erica said gently, "you have so much to be proud of. You're a lot younger than your father was when he—"

"Yes. I'm a huge success, money wise," he said dryly. "And money buys a lot of toys. In the short run, it buys a lot of women as well."

She was silent, not so much shocked as saddened by his attitude—for *his* sake.

"Who's kidding whom? That's the life I lead," he admitted quietly, and looked at her, his features impassive. "But women like you aren't just walking around, love."

"Sweetie," she said affectionately. His compliment, so out of the blue, had warmed her. More than that, she simply wanted to help Morgan if he needed help. But she also felt a strange sort of unease. Where was Kyle? She stood up and teasingly ordered Morgan ahead of her toward the kitchen. "What kind of lady do you expect to pick up in a singles bar anyway?"

If Kyle had been there, she wouldn't have hesitated to remain sitting with Morgan, to reach over and hug him, to urge him to talk and get his troubles off his chest. But Kyle wasn't there, and Morgan's eyes on her had been just a little more than friendly, more than just superficially appreciative. She felt a touch of guilt. It felt good to be wanted, to feel needed—and perhaps *she* needed *that* a bit too much right now, when Kyle seemed to be going out of his way to tell her he didn't need her, when in her heart she was afraid he didn't want her as he once had.

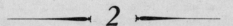

2

WHEN KYLE WALKED IN, Morgan was putting foil on the broiler for the steaks. Fresh mushrooms were simmering in soy sauce; the table had been set with china Erica hadn't used in months, and the second bottle of wine was on the table ready for pouring. In the last hour, Erica had turned all her attention toward urging Morgan out of his depression, and in the process had cheered herself. Candles on the table and a chance to dress up were part of that; for weeks she and Kyle had only snatched a bite in work clothes.

Her laughter was low and musical as she teased Morgan about his fastidious efforts in the kitchen, the effect of his elegant suit spoiled by the towel she'd given him to wear as an apron. When the front door opened, they were both hovering over the stove, with the bright lights of the kitchen haloing them in a little island of light.

Kyle stopped short, for a moment saying nothing, his eyes riveted on the two of them. There was a bag labeled McDonald's in his hand.

He was in shadow with the sunset behind him, his

13

black hair disheveled. Erica set down her fork with a clatter as she hurried down the three steps to the darkened living room and gave him a brilliant smile. There was only Kyle for that moment, as she went to him anticipating the change of mood that he, too, needed; anticipating his pleasure at seeing Morgan after so long; anticipating, in the most feminine ways, being with him again. It wasn't that Morgan suddenly didn't exist, that he shriveled in some imaginary way, that he was any less pleasant company, less good-looking, less fun to be with... but he *was* lesser, somehow. It was the weary man standing in the doorway, unmoving as she approached, for whom she felt an automatic, unstoppable surge of love.

She bounced up on tiptoe and curled her arms around his neck... yet the greeting kiss somehow ended differently than she had intended. Kyle's lips were cool and his eyes unreadable above hers, though for one instant his grip on her shoulders was so possessively tight that it hurt. He was looking past her, toward Morgan... Her smile suddenly froze on her face. She didn't try to understand his reaction; she was too busy handling her own. Not long ago he had welcomed her touch, openly courted her affectionate nature...

She buried the flicker of hurt. Two glasses of wine had muted that unnameable fear that he was tiring of her, that he no longer loved her. Pride insisted that she play it as normal. As she wanted it to be. She kept an arm around Kyle's narrow waist as they walked back up to the kitchen, reminding herself that he'd told her once she could not have looked sexier in that dress, and he had always loved her barefoot...

"Looks as if we won't be needing this," Kyle said dryly as he extricated himself from her embrace and set the McDonald's bag on the counter. "And it looks as if you two have been entertaining yourselves while I've been gone. Morgan—" The handshake was quick and automatic, Kyle's blue eyes bearing down on Morgan's brown ones with a strange deliberateness. "I've been expecting you, for some unknown reason. Actually, long before this. How've you been?"

"In trouble, regularly. You?"

"Morgan brought the steaks," Erica explained, feeling a sudden niggling worry that Kyle might have seen the fancy dinner and her dressy attire as efforts on her part to please Morgan. She appreciated the gesture of the McDonald's takeout supper more than she would have caviar; it was an acknowledgment that they were both sharing twelve-hour workdays. The worry passed. Morgan was Kyle's closest friend; Kyle could not possibly misunderstand. "You're just in time," she said brightly.

Morgan went out of his way to be entertaining throughout dinner. The wine flowed freely and the steaks were delicious; Erica and Kyle alternately praised and teased the chef. They were all more relaxed by the end of the meal. Erica mellowed as Kyle seemed to, feeling a glow of warmth inside every time her husband laughed at Morgan's deliberate and sometimes outrageous wit. It was the first genuine laughter she had seen in him in an age, and she noticed, too, as they rose from the dinner table, that the weariness and tension had left his features.

"I wish to hell you'd get tired of her," Morgan complained lazily to Kyle as he drew his arm around Erica's shoulders in a hug, urging her down the steps to the living room. "And if I haven't told you recently," he added to Erica, unvarnished deviltry in his brown eyes, "I'll give up the whole bit—wine, women, and song— the day you divorce him."

He meant Kyle to hear his comment. Morgan's nonsense was nothing new to either of them. "It's the best offer I've had all day," Erica assured him dryly. "If I weren't attracted to men with blue eyes—"

"Thanks," Morgan complained. "It's not as though I offer marriage every day of the week, and to be rejected because of—"

"You used to offer once a month, Morgan." She pressed

an affectionate kiss on his cheek to apologize for extricating herself from his hold. Banter was an integral method of communication for Morgan, and Erica expected it of him; yet for some reason the way he had held her, hip-to-hip, had grated in an unfamiliar manner. There was something so *deliberate,* so calculated about it. Not for the first time, she thought, remembering an earlier impression that Morgan wore his sexuality like a fashionable coat, bright in color to draw attention and a walking advertisement for the luxury of the fabric. He really couldn't help it.

Morgan nestled down in an easy chair with a contented sigh, surveying first Erica and then Kyle, who had followed just behind them. "You haven't said a word," he accused Kyle casually. "I take it you don't mind if I steal Erica away from you? You don't deserve her, you know."

Kyle stretched in the opposite chair, propping his long legs on an ottoman. His head rolled back as if the meal had depleted his last vestiges of energy, and he laced his fingers behind his neck. "Don't carry your kidding too far, okay, Morgan?" he said mildly. "I'd hate to have to worry about taking you seriously one of these days."

There was something in his tone ... Erica could not look at him suddenly. From out of nowhere, a strange friction had stolen into the room, and now it crackled around both men.

You're crazy, she told herself as she poured them coffee and set the cups on the table between them. She excused herself and went back to the kitchen to clean up. She did the job quietly, with half an ear to the conversation just below. The subject was politics while she washed and dried the dishes, and solar energy by the time she'd cleaned the counters, watered the hanging plants, and generally puttered about the kitchen.

The friction had disappeared. They talked the way they had always talked, man to man, with a firm respect for each other and a wary sharing of perspective. Wary, because the two men were competitive as all hell, a fact that continually amused Erica. She could not imagine having a woman friend with whom competition was the basis of the friendship; yet between the men it was fundamental.

She leaned over the counter when the chores were done, idly watching the scene below. Morgan was stretched out with his arms behind his head and one knee crossed over the other, a foot tapping rhythmically in the air. Morgan didn't know how to be still. When he talked, some part of his body talked as well. He was openly irritated when Kyle was right; Kyle was often right, and then Morgan's foot went back and forth like a hand fan on a hot day.

Kyle gave nothing away by such body language. His legs were stretched out, bare feet crossed at the ankles, the sleeves of his dark sweat shirt pushed up above his elbows revealing the thick dark hair that curled on his arms under the glow of the lamp. His face was in shadow; his jeans were stretched tight across his thighs. He was absolutely still except for his eyes, in which Erica saw a razor-sharp perception. He missed nothing. Kyle inhaled life, took everything in. Morgan picked up a single emotion at a time and lived it until the next one came along.

The differences between the two men had always intrigued her, yet Erica sighed, feeling a wave of fatigue as the hour grew late. She and Kyle had both been up since six. She moved down the three steps to settle on the couch with a cup of coffee, doubting that it would effectively keep her awake. Morgan smiled at her, immediately changing the conversation as he rose to offer her a glass of kirsch.

"I still haven't figured out what you two are up to," Morgan said to Kyle. "I knew you were coming back here after your father died and that it was going to take some time to take care of everything. I guess I just assumed that you meant to sell the place. Not . . . dig in here."

A moment passed before Kyle answered. For the first time, it occurred to Erica that Morgan had always been the one who was quick to confide, that Kyle had always been the one to bolster his friend in a crisis instead of the other way around. "I always di swear I'd never come back here," he admitted finally, leaning his head back. "But before my father died, I promised him . . . Hell, Shane, it doesn't matter." He esitated, masking a sudden brooding look as he stood up and turned away to pour himself a drink. "We're back here, indefinitely. That's all."

"But neither one of you can possibly want to settle in a town this small. I can't imagine what Erica finds to do here. And, Kyle, I thought you never got on with your father. You used to talk about this woodworking business as if you thought it was the pits."

"I used to think that way," Kyle agreed.

"You wanted money even more than I did. To get on top where no one could ever touch you. Success . . ."

"And I played that game for more than ten years." Kyle suddenly smiled wryly. "You and I always thought exactly alike, Shane. Get out of our way, world, because we're going up! You were in competition with your father; I was running from the life my father led. It doesn't matter. Maybe everyone has to get out of the race at some point."

Morgan stared at him. "So you're saying you just want a break, then. That I can understand. I thought you were talking about living here permanently."

Kyle said very quietly, "I don't know." *Leave it,* his tone of voice urged. *Now.*

Erica sipped her kirsch, unsettled by Morgan's probing. She knew nothing of a promise Kyle had made to his father, but she was acutely conscious that he had said nothing to Morgan about the debts Joel had left for them to pay off. More than that, she could see in Kyle the almost imperceptible change that seemed to come over

him whenever someone mentioned his father. A slight
stiffening of his shoulders, a chill replacing the warm
and vibrant expression in his eyes ... As though he were
haunted by guilt, she thought, when that just couldn't
be. Kyle had been a wonderful son to Joel, generous and
concerned. They had lived some distance apart, of
course ...

"... covered with stain and her hands full of paint
thinner!" Morgan was laughing.

"I can't keep her out of it." Kyle's brooding blue eyes
flickered to hers. "You should see some of the projects
she's taken on."

"*Now* I'm beginning to get the picture," Morgan said,
grinning. "The lady's the monkey wrench you hadn't
expected to find in the works, Kyle? Maybe it's the image
of raising kids in the country—"

"I'm here," Erica reminded them pleasantly.

"The lady's loyal. But then, in the first throes of
idealism people are always filled with enthusiasm," Kyle
continued to Morgan.

"I beg your pardon—"

But Morgan was staring deliberately at Kyle. "That
will last until she misses her spring trip to Paris to buy
clothes. The swimming pool in the back yard, the country
club. Everything she grew up to expect. You can't give
it to her here, can you, Kyle?"

Kyle finished his drink, looking at Morgan, not both-
ering to answer. Erica felt a knot twist in the pit of her
stomach. Morgan's tone was light; he couldn't possibly
know what a knife wound he had just inflicted on Kyle.

"Morgan," she said flatly, "I have never in my life
gone to Paris to buy clothes."

"No," Kyle agreed quietly, "it was New York you
and your mother went to for your shopping sprees. Twice
a year." He stood up and stretched. "Maybe it's time we
all called it a night. Morgan, you're going to be here
through the morning?"

Morgan shook his head, standing, too. "I've got to get back pretty early. This stopover was stolen time as it was."

The two men talked a few minutes longer, while Erica got up to take the glasses to the kitchen, then fetched linens to make the couch up as a bed for Morgan. Her stomach was still tied up in knots. The two of them always played the old men-against-the-women war when the trio was together; usually it amused her. It didn't tonight. They both made it sound as though she valued material things above all else. In the past, she knew they had been very important to her, and yes, occasionally she missed the freedom to buy a steak instead of hamburger or to have fresh strawberries out of season. She was no saint. But she didn't miss those biannual shopping expeditions, or the swank house in Florida, or Beluga caviar. And her new life offered certain riches she had never had before—the thrill of building something together, a sense of accomplishment and satisfaction in her own work, the pleasure of being an active participant in their marriage, in their...life. It was an opportunity to share a life as they never had before.

If Kyle wanted her there. But ever since they moved, he had fought every single thing she tried to do to help him. For Erica, it was like discovering a rainbow that disappeared every time she came close. She saw the chance to achieve a real depth that had been missing in their marriage before; yet each time she went in search of it, Kyle—*her* Kyle—disappeared, walled up inside himself.

She finished making up the couch. The two men had collapsed in their chairs again, and were once more discussing solar energy. Wearily, she sat on the carpet beside Kyle, leaning her head back against his knee. She was frankly dead on her feet, but she was not going to bed without him. No way. The stiff posture of pride he'd erected as a barrier between them made her ache with the desire to bridge the gap.

She heard none of their conversation. Absently, Kyle's fingers were playing with her silky hair as he continued talking, lifting and smoothing the tresses with gentle fingertips. His touch was so soft it brought a quiver inside, a sensual desire to lean her head back even farther and bare her throat for him. Was she perhaps too sensitive to his every mood, making a mountain out of the molehill of his recent indifference? But that sensitivity was a gift as well, when Kyle's slightest touch could evoke such an incredible languid sensuality from deep within her.

"If nothing else, you could generate power for a hot-water system that way. I was reading..."

"Your wife always did have eyes too big for her face when she was tired, Kyle," Morgan interrupted abruptly. "I think Erica's about to fall asleep against your leg. Maybe it *is* time we called it a night."

Erica raised her head, startled at the tone of his voice. Morgan was staring at her with a strange expression—displeasure, something tight and controlled in the set of his jaw. She felt an odd kind of embarrassment, as if she were a teenager caught by a parent in some intimacy, when of course there was nothing like that. She glanced back at Kyle, who was viewing Morgan with narrowed eyes, his face too much in shadow for her to discern his exact expression. Kyle's hand suddenly tightened possessively on her shoulder, and then he urged her to her feet with a pat on the back. "Up we go."

"I made up the couch," Erica started to tell Morgan, "but if you need anything..."

"You ought to know I can take care of myself after all this time," he chided, but there was no playfulness in his voice, no warmth, and she sensed that his eyes followed the two of them as they made their way up the winding stairs. Erica felt the hardness of his gaze, almost as if it were a hex. But that, of course, was ridiculous, a wild fancy brought on by exhaustion... and fear.

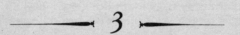

3

THE CARPETED SPIRAL staircase that led to the loft, with its wrought-iron banister, never failed to give Erica the illusion of climbing to another world. Which it was, when she reached the top.

The beamed ceiling stretched in a long inverted V the full length of the large room. The far wall was all glass, allowing the moon and stars to cast a shimmering light on the dark carpet. There was none of the clutter or cheerfulness of the room below; the mood here was one of peace and privacy. They'd built the bed on a carpeted platform; to the right of the stairs was Kyle's private area—bookshelves, a recessed desk space; to the left of the stairs was her own niche, with recessed cabinets where she stored her needlework and other personal projects. Both areas were separated from the bedroom proper by hand-scrolled screens that could easily be put aside. Quiet colors and textures made the loft a haven that contrasted sharply to the vibrant hues and energy of the downstairs areas.

Kyle moved past her to the bathroom, and Erica absently wandered to the dresser to take out a nightgown. She'd switched on the lamp by the bed when she came up for Morgan's bedding; now she switched it off and moved to the glass wall.

The bushes were trembling below in a night breeze. A gnarled old elm reached up to stroke a light-leafed branch against the window. Fleeting clouds were playing a game of chase across a midnight sky, the moon a stark lemony crescent behind them.

The country road in front of the house rarely saw a passing car at this hour. The town of Three Oaks was only a ten-minute drive, and it was Three Oaks and a half-dozen other small towns like it that brought in their business, though Madison, the state capital, was not too far away. In the short time she'd lived here, Wisconsin had impressed Erica by its lack of skyscrapers and the absence of the hustle-bustle that went with them. Oh, there was industry from Green Bay down to Milwaukee, but that wasn't the *flavor* of the state.

The flavor was country and country towns, where European immigrants had settled some generations before with their crafts and their customs and their desire to establish roots and live in peace. The Wisconsin landscape, with its winding roads and endless woods and streams, offered shelter, a gentle privacy that had changed very little for generations. In Erica's imagination, Wisconsin was all lush greens, not the arid leaf color she associated with Florida. The nights were more velvet here, the earth a rich dark color . . . It mattered somehow. The place had had a sensual appeal for her, a feeling of rightness, even from the beginning.

She heard Kyle behind her and turned to him with the nightgown still in her hand. In the darkness, she could hear him moving toward the bed, drawing down the sheets. Absently, she reached behind her to unsnap the hooks of her smocked dress. "Kyle?"

"Mmm?"

He was exhausted; she knew that; it was the worst of

times to bring up anything that mattered. Still, she couldn't quite let it go. "When you were talking to Morgan," she asked tentatively, "what did you mean? What was the promise you made to your father?"

"It doesn't matter, Erica."

But it did—to her. Leaning back in the shadows, she waited. Kyle shifted restlessly against the pillows. "My father told me the McCrery name meant nothing to me," he said neutrally. "He died lonely, because of my pride. I misjudged him badly over the years..."

She shook her head violently, though he couldn't see the gesture in the darkness. "Kyle, you were good to him," she protested. "I know you lived far away, but that...just happens. You called; you always saw that he was cared for; you sent him money. Morgan told me once that you even built this house; you were in school, working three jobs, and he thought you were crazy to come back up here that summer... And you stayed with him that whole month before he died—"

"I left the minute I was eighteen and never really came back. I knew I was all he had. He knew how I felt; he told me so before he died. The respect of one man for another—I never had it for him, and I was wrong. But I didn't know how much it mattered that he didn't have it for me."

"I don't understand," Erica said, her voice growing angry. "Kyle, I don't *have* to understand. He was wrong." She slipped the dress over her head impatiently. She shivered a little, but the cool night air was like silk on her skin. Moonlight brushed the delicate lines of her collarbone and shoulders, her long, slim thighs. Her mind was racing, trying to find the right words to say to Kyle, trying to understand how and why his feelings for his father had so painfully changed him from the man she had married.

Her hair fell in a slow-sweeping red-gold arc as she bent to remove her panties. When she straightened, her entire profile was illuminated, her skin tinged with the satin sheen of moonlight. "Listen," she began.

He was out of bed, moving up behind her. He pulled her back against his chest, nuzzling her hair back with his chin so he could kiss the hollow in her shoulder. "We can't have you standing in that window, love. Anyone passing by would undoubtedly have an accident. The look of you—that natural sensual grace of yours—could well cause a five-car pile-up." His lips dipping for her shoulders again, he added gravely, "We can't have that on your conscience."

She remembered that low, vibrant tone of his all too well; her heart instinctively changed beats. She felt warmer suddenly, in a way she hadn't felt warm for weeks, loving the feel of his callused hands on the smooth skin of her stomach. "There's never anyone out here at this hour. Except," she qualified, "raccoons." There were two tiny beacons that could have been raccoon eyes in the distance, bright pinpricks behind a giant oak.

"They'll have to go. This is my view," he asserted, and she chuckled, turning in his arms to face him.

He was naked. It seemed a century since she'd felt free simply to run her hands over his arms, over the smooth contours of his shoulders. "It never occurred to me that you might be jealous of raccoons," she remarked innocently. "Do you have the same mistrust of foxes? Squirrels?"

He took a nip of the tender skin of her neck. "I'm jealous of the air that touches you, Erica. A well-kept secret." His voice was so low she could barely hear it. His weariness seemed to have disappeared. The vibrant sheen in his eyes caressed her as intimately as his hands.

She hadn't forgotten what they had been discussing; it mattered too much...yet she closed her eyes for a second at his seductive touch, savoring the sweet rush of heat in her limbs. This was Kyle again, not the stranger whose distant manner so frightened her. She craved his warmth, hungered for closeness, yet she wanted a mating of more than bodies. "Kyle..."

He pushed her gently toward the bed. The sheets felt oddly cool against her warmed skin. "Don't talk." He leaned over her, smoothing back her hair, stealing the pillow away from her head so she lay flat and vulnerable. His lips brushed hers fleetingly, his thumb tenderly caressing her cheek. "No more talk," he whispered fiercely. "I know your loyalty, Erica. God, I never meant to drag you into this." His mouth suddenly claimed hers, with a searing pressure of urgency and hunger. "When I first met you, you were like sunlight in a very dark world," he murmured. "You've never changed, not for me. Sunlight and softness, elusive and fragile; I wanted to protect you, shelter you, in a way you can't possibly understand. I need you as I need breath . . ."

"Kyle . . ." It wasn't his words so much as the desperate intensity she sensed behind them. It was the words he wasn't saying, didn't know how to say; she felt frightened suddenly. As if he were talking about something that was irretrievably lost already . . . Fiercely, his lips settled on hers again, stifling the words she needed to say, and in spite of herself she felt a quiver of longing run through her like quicksilver. He was part of the night, her Kyle, part of every sensual dream she had ever had. Suddenly, it only made sense to reach out, to cleave to him, to try to bridge the distance between them at a level more basic than talk.

His eyes burned down to hers in the darkness in a way that made her tremble inside. He shifted still closer, pinning her with the solid weight of his thigh as the feather-light touch of his fingers skimmed over the delicate line of her collarbone. Then his head bent, his teeth nipping at her soft neck with a roughness that teased, his palm sweeping down the length of her, taking in breast and stomach and thigh. He knew her well. The contrast of rough and soft, gentle and fierce, ignited the most primitive needs, unleashed the kaleidoscope of fantasies secreted within her. Her mind spun in sweet, fierce splendor as she reached for him.

His hand clasped hers before she could touch him. "Let me. Just let me," he murmured. In a light hold, he pinned her wrists above her head with one hand. His lips parted hers, his tongue stealing inside first to taste and savor, then to drain her special private flavor. She felt her blood race, a delicious sense of helplessness flooding through her that was potently erotic. His free hand teased at that forced submissiveness, pirating down slowly to knead one pillow-soft breast until it swelled and the peak firmed and hardened for him, pouting when his palm deserted it to move down her ribs, then lower.

The late hour, the long day of work, the tension he'd worn all day like an extra layer of clothes...he was in no hurry. For long moments, he seemed mesmerized by the play of moonlight on her skin, by the hollows and shadows the night created. Then his palm smoothed over the flat satin of her stomach and down to her thigh, so slowly that a whispery shudder seemed to take over her whole body. She longed to touch as well as be touched. She could feel his arousal throbbing against her thigh, could hear the change in his breathing. To share was to love, and he'd taught her all about that; passivity no longer pleased her. Desperately, she wanted to give as well as take, and her hands twisted...

His wrist tightened on them. "This one's for you..."

"No," she whispered. "For *us*. Please, Kyle..."

Again his mouth covered hers, drowning her words and her senses. Petal-soft, his fingertips grazed the sensitive skin of her inner thighs, his touch as tantalizingly light as his kiss was possessively firm. His lips gradually relinquished hers, only to trail lazy kisses down her throat and neck. Restlessly, she tossed her head from side to side as his mouth settled hungrily on one breast. His tongue lapped over and over until the nipple peaked and ached; she could feel her hands curl into fists above her head. "Kyle..."

He hushed her in velvet whispers. As his lips feasted at her breasts, his free hand sought the silky down of her

womanhood. The more responsive she was, the more
slowly he explored, savoring every possible inch of flesh
as if this were the first time, the last time . . . as if her
pleasure were the only thing that mattered. She drew in
her breath when his lips touched her thighs. She felt
insanely vulnerable, his plundering tongue against her
flesh a shocking rough-smooth sensation that laid open
a need that came from her soul. She heard a feverish
moan in her throat. He whispered endearments to her . . .

Finally, he shifted, locking their bodies together before she could even draw breath. His warmth was suddenly everywhere, surrounding her; his powerful
rhythm—a rhythm designed to block out mind and heartache and time—was inescapably her rhythm, too. He
knew exactly the cadence of movement to take her soaring; no one else in the world knew her like that, understood how to take that surge of wildness and spin it
completely out of control. "Please . . ."

There was a feverish glaze of almost-tears in her eyes
when he finally freed her hands, and she desperately
clutched at the damp silk of his back, holding on, holding
him with her. She felt his hand suddenly over her mouth
to muffle her helpless cry when her body seemed to turn
liquid. Liquid gold.

When it was over, he touched her cheek with his palm,
soothing away the hint of tears. He tucked her inside the
curve of his shoulder in the darkness. For a time, their
breathing was labored; then his quieted as he fell asleep.

Erica lay still, trembling, for a long time. Sleep should
have come instantly, yet it eluded her. The sensual, le-
thargic aftermath of love faded slowly; finally, she moved
from beside Kyle's sleeping form and groped her way
to the chair in her corner of the room.

He had an incredible power in his hands, her virile
lover. He'd had it from the beginning; for her there had
never been a question of withholding a response from
him, of inhibitions or hesitation or shyness. She loved
the lover as well as the man, but there'd been something

different tonight. He hadn't wanted her to touch him; he hadn't wanted to be loved in return. He gave so much, but at the very moment he himself most needed loving. She knew it as an instinct, felt it in her heart...

Erica got up, found a long, cream-colored robe, put it on, and curled up in the chair. The night was silent except for Kyle's breathing, and once the whispery hooting of an owl. Erica sat in the chair, wide-eyed, tearless, frightened. Kyle's love play so closely paralleled other things that were happening in their marriage, the way he so often closed himself off to her...

She had believed their marriage was perfect—until Joel McCrery died and that tragedy had uncovered depths of feeling she hadn't known existed, emotions and capacities in herself that had never been tapped. Their changed circumstances had given her the opportunity to stand by Kyle, to fight for something together, to change and grow with him... Yet while her love for him had grown, his feelings for her seemed to have diminished. He had shut her off when she had tried to talk. Now, when she wanted to touch...

She didn't know what to do, what to think, what she was supposed to feel. She hurt, she suffered—it was a raw, confused, nameless sensation. Unwillingly, she closed her eyes in exhaustion, and finally made her way back to bed.

Erica cracked an egg against the counter and plopped it gently into a pot of boiling water, bounced a slice of bread into the toaster, snatched up knife, fork, and napkin, and set them on the counter in front of Morgan. In another few seconds, she had two cups of coffee poured, an apple sliced, and a glass of juice waiting for Morgan. The poached egg was ready by the time the slowest toaster in the Midwest noisily popped up one browned slice of bread. She handed Morgan's plate to him as she perched on a stool on the opposite side of the counter. "Now eat," she ordered as she picked up an apple slice

and motioned to his plate with it. "It'll give you something to do besides bore that dead-man stare of yours
into my back. Didn't you sleep well?"

"I just don't understand how anyone can move so fast
first thing in the morning." Morgan's blond hair was
rumpled, and he had put on his suit pants but nothing
else. A dangling St. Christopher medal hung from his
tanned neck, and on one hand he sported a full-carat
sapphire. High-class disheveled, Erica privately labeled
him. As much as she cared for him, she was in no mood
to entertain anyone this morning, much less Morgan,
who seemed determined to study the hollows of fatigue
beneath her eyes.

"Honey, those jeans couldn't get much tighter."

"Oh, hush." The jeans were old, white, and ideal for
applying varnish to a roll-top desk. Her navy top was
another paint-spattered T-shirt, and today, in deference
to Morgan, she wore a bra.

Kyle was gone. When Erica awakened, the bedroom
had been empty; there had been no sound or sight of
him. A squirrel had been chattering outside the glass
wall, a pair of robins had been pecking at the dew-
drenched grass for a gourmet breakfast of worms, and
the brilliant early morning sunshine had promised a lovely
day; it had all been rather annoying. When one's life was
falling apart, nature should at least have the courtesy to
provide a mucky, rainy day. Instead, a seven-thirty sunlight was streaming into the bright kitchen, and Morgan's
brown eyes were steady on hers like admiring beacons.
Worse, he was already full of his particular brand of
nonsense.

"One small smile, eked out after three sips of coffee
and an apple," he observed. "I think it was the lady who
had a little problem sleeping last night."

"A little," she admitted. "Oh, Lord!" She glanced
furtively at the front door as they both heard a scratching
from behind them, and in a second she was off the stool,
grabbing a bowl from the cupboard and opening the back

door. The cat stopped scratching instantly and leaped in to tangle herself around Erica's legs as she reached out to get the milk from the refrigerator and pour some into the bowl. "We will *not* mention this to Kyle," she said severely to Morgan.

"I take it Kyle doesn't like cats." Morgan leaned back with his cup in hand, grinning broadly. "Does the thing have mange, or has it just been in an accident?"

"Not you, too!" Erica protested. "Hurry," she urged the creature. The cat was a skinny faded calico, with strangely long legs and tufts of fur at intervals. When the bowl was empty of milk, she curled around Erica's legs again. Erica crouched down, stroking her. "What could I do?" she said helplessly to Morgan. "She comes every day."

"You don't suppose it's because you feed her, do you?" Morgan suggested helpfully.

"She was starving!"

"So are all those children in China."

"Morgan!" she said disgustedly as she shooed the cat back out the door.

"Your secret's safe with me," he assured her with a grin. "Although you're kidding yourself if you think Kyle doesn't already know you're a sucker for lost causes. Now quit jumping around for two seconds and sit down with your coffee. I want to talk with you."

"What about?" she asked. She washed out the empty bowl and put it away.

"What's wrong?" he asked abruptly.

"Pardon?"

He sighed impatiently. "I've known Kyle for twelve years and you for better than nine. Kyle looks as if he's carrying the world on his shoulders, and you, love, are more tense than that cat could ever be."

"Nothing's exactly wrong," she protested, as she drank her coffee. She sipped too quickly, the scalding liquid fiery on her tongue, meeting his probing eyes only for an instant over the rim of the cup before she looked away.

She was not good at lying, and Morgan had been a friend for too long for her simply to tell him to mind his own business. "Kyle's just terribly tired," she said finally.

"So he's driving himself to the limit. Why? You two chose to come here. You left a successful business..."

"Yes," Erica interrupted rapidly. "And this one is doing well, too, Morgan. It's just that we started out with so many..."

"Debts," Morgan supplied smoothly.

She had never intended to say that, but she could tell from the expression on Morgan's face that he had already guessed.

"I would have to be a fool not to have realized that there was more to the move here than Kyle's sudden love affair with wood," Morgan continued. "Woodworking may have been in his blood for generations, but it sure as hell didn't show up until now. So how bad was it, Erica?"

Totally unhappy with herself, Erica drained the coffee cup and turned away to set it in the sink. Kyle had chosen not to tell Morgan about their circumstances; knowing that made her feel helplessly disloyal. But Morgan *was* Kyle's best friend; perhaps another man's perspective was exactly what Kyle needed. Maybe he should talk out his feelings with Morgan. Taking a breath she said quietly, "Joel didn't have any health insurance. The doctors performed open-heart surgery three times to try to get his heart going, but it was too badly damaged. He spent months in the intensive care unit... and before that he had bought thousands of dollars' worth of lumber, none of it paid for. Other debts he seemed to have just accumulated... Of course, toward the end, Joel wasn't well enough to work," Erica said awkwardly. "But in the meantime, it couldn't have been a worse time for Kyle to sell *his* business, with the economy so sluggish. He had a lot of capital out, or something; he'd just started another little plant..." Her voice trailed off. Then, chin lifted, she determinedly met Morgan's eyes. "We're out from under now," she assured him. "For that matter, when I see the way Kyle works with a piece of wood, when I see what he can do with his hands . . . I wonder how he could ever have been really happy with a suit-and-tie sort of life. You wouldn't believe what he's been able to accomplish in six months, but there's been so much stress . . ." She took a breath. "Perhaps if you talked to him, Morgan . . ."

"That was a hell of a pair of shoes to leave you," Morgan said abruptly, as if he hadn't even heard her suggestion. "But is that all that's wrong, Erica?"

His sharp brown eyes looked intensely into hers. "Of course that's all," she said.

"Is it?"

She nodded nervously. "I like working with Kyle."

"I still don't understand, Erica. Kyle's one story, but you're another. You can't possibly like it here, a tiny country town with nothing to do. It's not just the lack of entertainment, but security, everything you grew up accustomed to . . ."

He was like a dog worrying a bone. All she wanted was for Morgan to give Kyle moral support—as Kyle had done for him a thousand times. "Morgan, we *both* like it here. We like working with wood. And Kyle has roots here . . ."

"You don't," Morgan said bluntly.

"I have Kyle." But it sounded wrong, suddenly. She wasn't at all sure she *did* have Kyle anymore.

"Yes." Morgan stood up, lazily stretching, the silver metal on his chest glittering in the morning sun. "Well, kiddo, I've got to hit the road. This time, though, it's not going to be such a long lapse between visits."

"Super," she said brightly, relieved he'd changed the subject. "You know we're always glad to see you."

He snatched at her hand as she moved past him. "So give us a good-bye kiss to tide us over," he said swiftly.

She raised her cheek obediently for his peck and instead found his mouth on hers, the still-warm aroma of coffee mixed with a fractionally too intense pressure of lips. Somewhat startled, she stared up at him, as if searching his face for some assurance that it hadn't been the kind of kiss it seemed to be. His hands lingered on her shoulders, and then he dropped his arms to his sides, pure Morgan in his cool expression, the usual hint of deviltry in his eyes. "You know, I've been waiting nine years for you to find some fault with that Irishman," he teased.

Somehow it did not have the playful ring that it should have had. Still, she found the smile for him that she supposed should be on her face. Morgan was just...Morgan. He'd be stealing from the cookie jar when he was ninety.

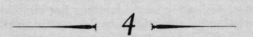

4

A WALK IN the sunshine inevitably lifted Erica's spirits. A squirrel was scampering across the dew-drenched grass, chattering to her the entire time it took her to get to the shop. The brisk morning air cleared the mental cobwebs, and she mounted the steps still smiling at the little animal's antics.

Inside, she paused, inhaling the smells of the trade with a sensual pleasure. Sawdust and turpentine and wood and varnish...not exactly the smells to appeal to a romantic nature. But they appealed to hers, she thought fleetingly.

Kyle had rarely talked of his family or his past. It hadn't mattered until she knew they were moving here, and then she'd put together some of his rare family anecdotes and historical information she'd gathered at the library. Particularly in the mid-1800's, Europeans had flooded to the Midwest, seeking relief from famines and military rule. They weren't urban dwellers but simple country people, wanting only to pursue the lives they knew—farming or trades—with a decent chance for their families survival. People who knew hardship but still had the courage and strength to follow a dream...

The McCrerys were dairy farmers and carpenters—and probably horse thieves, Kyle had told her dryly. Woodworking was their craft, and a sizable business was built up by the third generation; in the fourth—Joel's—came mass production. Homemade wood products were too expensive then; there was always a place for a carpenter, but if a man had need to create...

Erica had learned that Joel was an intensely creative man, that he had never been happy simply putting hammer to board. Nothing else made sense as to why the business was such a mess when they first came here. She'd had such a wonderful romantic picture of the place in her mind. History, roots, Wisconsin greenery, the gentle melancholy she'd sensed in Joel, the cottage nestled among the trees, a place where people had found peace for generations in a quiet, private way...

Absently, Erica smoothed her palm down the finely sanded grain of a red cedar plank, and then bent down to smell the fresh tang of the new wood. Six months ago, she'd walked into this room one morning when Kyle was gone, and found rusted tools, lumber haphazardly stacked, filthy windows, and the smell of neglect and waste. Her expectation of romance had evaporated in an uncharacteristic sensation of fear. This was not what she had pictured. Kyle could not conceivably have grown up here; Kyle, who had such a love of space and privacy, who hated clutter and had no tolerance at all for waste and neglect.

Finding the little pigeonhole of an office was the next shock. Much of the paperwork was incomprehensible to her, but she understood enough. The night before she'd served crab for which she'd paid fifteen dollars a pound; Kyle had affectionately encouraged her to stay out of the shop, to spend whatever she liked to make the cottage livable. Carpet, linens, furniture...

She was so used to a certain kind of life that she'd

never thought about it, never realized how Kyle had always sheltered and even pampered her, indulging her every whim, ferreting out wishes she hadn't even known she had. She hadn't confronted him that day—she couldn't. Uppermost in her mind had been her own sudden and overwhelming feeling of inadequacy. For how long had she behaved like a mistress instead of a wife? It hadn't occurred to Kyle, apparently, to level with her about their changed circumstances. Did he think she wouldn't *see*, wouldn't understand?

She hadn't then and didn't now understand his anger when he first found her washing windows, taking on projects. Obviously, he didn't have time for the antiques, and those were less a matter of skill than time, patience, and work. And in spite of all the problems they'd had lately, she had slowly and almost unconsciously built up a love affair with wood that was almost equal to her husband's.

With her hands stuck in her back pockets, she wandered toward Kyle's shop, a long, narrow side room that ran the length of the building. Every chisel had its place, the power tools were protected and hung on hooks; excellent lighting had been installed; and the wood lathe gleamed like dull pewter from its proper oiling and care. Kyle had changed so much, so quickly... She would have been beaten just looking at the shop when she first saw it. He had savored the challenge. The market for handmade wooden products had supposedly disappeared after mass production became common, but people seemed to be tired of houses that looked alike, perhaps were again beginning to value things that endured. In a plastic world where so little was natural, wood had qualities to offer—it was lasting, beautiful, real. A chair unearthed from the attic and refinished would last another thirty years, and no one else had another like it; a wooden cradle could be a link between one generation and the next, lovingly passed on as people used to do, because they had the sense and sensitivity to do it...

She noticed a massive piece of mahogany in the shape of a sunburst at the far end of Kyle's workbench and wandered toward it, curious as to what he was working on. Her hands slipped out of her pockets as she neared. She'd never seen it before. The huge sunburst was nearly finished. The sun's points were smooth and sharp and exact, but Kyle was hand-chiseling the center into a three-dimensional design to create the effect of leaping flames. The longer she stared, the more fascinated she became. There seemed to be a face in the flames, a cameo hidden in the intricate work.

The flames looked alive, with the illusion of a woman's profile . . . *she* was the woman, the sun itself—life, warmth, radiance. Shoulder-length hair swirled and became part of the fire, almost as if it had color. Reverently, Erica touched the arc of one perfect sunpoint.

She felt a sharp hand connect with her backside before she was whirled off-balance. "You didn't see that." Kyle's arms hooked around her shoulders, preventing her from turning and seeing it again. His eyes hinted at turquoise this morning and had that very private brightness she saw only when he was working . . . or seducing.

Either way, she relished it, grinning up at him. "I didn't see it." Well, that wasn't going to work. "Kyle, that sunburst is the most beautiful thing I've ever seen. I don't know when you could possibly have found the time to work on something like that—"

"I have been working exclusively on cabinets for one Jonas Henry."

"I mean the sunburst—"

He kissed her forehead. "There isn't any sunburst. I haven't the least idea what you're talking about."

"Kyle, I—"

"If you're smart, lady, you'll keep in mind that you didn't see a thing. Unless you want a bonfire for your birthday."

She nodded rapidly. "I never saw a thing."

For that she rated a single swift kiss on the lips, far

too short. Her hands lingered on his shoulders. His black hair gleamed under the fluorescent lights, last night's sleep not sufficient to erase the hollows beneath his eyes. They didn't matter. Those hollows only accented his good looks, those beautiful eyes of his... Yet his eyes changed suddenly as his hands tightened around her waist and then released her. "Erica, last year on your birthday I gave you an emerald..."

"And it was lovely," she said quietly. "But this—this is worth more, Kyle, can't you see that?"

He lifted one eyebrow. *"What's* worth more?" he demanded.

"Nothing. Nothing. I didn't see a thing!"

"And for that peek, it'll be a long time before I forgive you." Another short spank on her backside somehow ended as an intimate pat instead. "For once, Erica, I have to urge you back into your own workroom."

"You're *not* trying to get rid of me, are you?" she asked teasingly, but she headed for the door. The oak desk was waiting for varnishing, and Kyle had his own work to do.

Five minutes later, she was kneeling on the tarp in the back room, the can of varnish open beside her and her gloved hand holding a brush. An hour passed before she lifted her head, startled to find Kyle standing in the doorway. He was a different man again; she didn't know what had happened. The turquoise was gone from his eyes, and the brooding look was back; his sinewy shoulders were taut beneath the navy shirt he wore.

For a moment, he said nothing, his eyes skimming over the pieces of furniture waiting for their turn after she finished the desk: a Jenny Lind couch, an old cradle, a huge antique spinning wheel some farmer had unearthed from his attic. Her own advertising had brought in that business, and she was itching to get at her work. But Kyle's eyes were cold, shifting from the furniture to his wife, kneeling on the rough tarp in a frayed T-shirt and paint-spattered jeans. A bleakness seemed to come over his features, masked quickly by that steel-hard look she'd come to fear. "Kyle?"

"Erica, did you ask Morgan to come here?"

The question seemed to come out of nowhere. "Of course not." She half smiled. "I can't remember a time Morgan ever waited for an invitation to visit us. Every time he feels a little restless, he just zeroes in."

Kyle stared out the window. "Wisconsin happens to be a little farther than Florida, as far as just dropping in goes."

"He explained that. The Shanes' business is expanding, and the Midwest is the direction it's going." And since Morgan's family was in small aircraft, it had always been a simple matter for Morgan to fly wherever he wanted to go. Erica frowned. Kyle knew all of that. She wasn't sure what he was trying to say. "You would rather he hadn't come?" she questioned. "And I thought you would be so glad to see him after all this time. You two have been friends for so long..."

"Yes. And we shared a lot for a very long time." The conversation on that subject was evidently over. Kyle strode forward, crouched down beside her, and took the brush from her hands. His stroke was the stroke of a lover, sensitive and sure, as he finished the side she had been working on and viewed the result with a critical eye. "Your work is perfect, Erica. Exactly right to bring out the texture of the wood."

Her heart played John Philip Sousa under his praise. "It's a beautiful piece to work on." She promptly forgot about Morgan.

"And you're my beautiful lady." He leaned over to kiss the tip of her nose, and then handed back her brush. Standing up again, he watched as she finished the last side.

She was promptly unnerved. For one thing, Kyle never stood idle; for another, he never watched what she did; and for another...one of these years of marriage she was going to stop feeling that butterfly reaction to the sheer sex appeal of her husband. It was ridiculous, of course. She knew exactly what Kyle looked like in every mood and type of dress. Still, her heart soared at the proud way he always held his shoulders, was painfully aware of the way his dark shirt showed off his bronzed skin, savored the intense blue of his eyes.

"You want lessons?" she inquired finally, tongue-in-cheek.

He chuckled. "I want your attention. When you're done, Erica—God knows I hate an interruption. But this morning...I just want to show you something."

Her eyebrows rose in surprise. "Why didn't you say anything?" She was finished in short order, though Kyle took the brushes from her hands and cleaned them before she had the chance to do it herself. "What do you want to show me?"

He shook his head. "Not yet." He swung an arm around her shoulders as they left the old building, both of them blinking to adjust to the sudden bright sunlight. She could sense just from the feel of Kyle's hand that his earlier, brighter mood had returned. He led her back to the house, through the front door, and up to the kitchen, where he detached himself only long enough to raid the cookie jar.

"I see. We both only have a thousand things to do. I can certainly understand why you wanted to show me chocolate-chip cookies," she said pleasantly. "I haven't seen one in nearly two days—"

He pushed her, none too gently, out the front door ahead of him. "The talk we're about to have couldn't take place without your cookies," he informed her. "We're nearly out," he added sadly.

"Is that supposed to be a less than subtle hint...?"

"Certainly not. You think I'm some kind of male chauvinist, demanding that my woman be in the kitchen all the time?" He hesitated. "I have heard that cookie withdrawal can be one of the most painful experiences known to man. Some people even die from it."

"They do."

"You're not doubting me?"

"Whatever would make you think that?"

"This morning, lady, I don't need anyone to doubt me." He led her about a hundred yards east of the old workshop building. The McCrery property was surrounded by woods; the clearing where he stopped was overgrown with wild flowers and tall grasses, and bordered on the road. Since she saw it every morning, she couldn't imagine why he'd brought her here. "Sit," he urged her.

"Here?"

"Okay. Stand." He was brushing the cookie crumbs from his hands, looking more relaxed than she had seen him in an age.

But the soft grass was suddenly very inviting. She sat down, pulling her knees up to her chest, watching him with mixed amusement and curiosity. Kyle hadn't shown his whimsical side in months; she loved it.

Kyle paced out about twenty yards from her and then stopped. "The people will come in here." He gestured. "For a display area—your arena, Erica. No more of that hands-and-knees nonsense in the back room. Not that you have to do anything at all, but this job will at least give you time for the other things you like to do—"

"Kyle—"

"The antiques will be off to the side. Here, I think. Lumber stocked here . . ."

It took her a moment to catch on. Kyle was pacing out an imaginary building, three times the size of the original shop. Where a person could walk in and find anything he or she wanted in the way of wood, whether it was new cabinetry or a refinished antique, a handcrafted headboard or a do-it-yourself project. Mesmerized, Erica listened, catching Kyle's enthusiasm as he talked. From zebra wood to teak, he was lining up the imaginery shelves, stocking only the finest lumber, the best available tools and implements for anything anyone could want in the way of wood.

"Well?" he demanded finally, as he settled down beside her, snatched up a long strand of grass and stuck it lazily between his teeth.

"I love it," she said warmly. I love you, she wanted to say. "It's a terrific idea, Kyle. And in time..."

"Next week."

"Pardon?"

The teasing turquoise faded from Kyle's eyes; he took out the strand of grass and tossed it aside. "The bank likes the idea, Erica. Of drawing in all the separate markets under one roof. At the rate we're going, we'll be out of the red in a month—and left precisely nowhere. Unless we expand, our business will only eke out a middling income." At her startled expression, he said quietly, "I merely had to show the bank what we've already done. I researched the markets myself, Erica. We can bring in people from a good distance by producing something unique, something they can't get anywhere else—"

"Darling, it isn't that." Her lips felt dry. The volatile tension she'd seen in him so often lately seemed to vibrate from every pore. "Kyle, you're driving yourself so hard. You haven't had a full eight hours' sleep in months, and to take this on so soon—"

Restlessly, he lurched back up to his feet, motioning toward a spot behind the house. "I figure we can have a swimming pool back there in a few years. Maybe not as large as the one your father has, but certainly large enough to cool us off on a day like today. After that—"

"Kyle, I don't want a damn swimming pool. I like what we have." She stood up, too, suddenly feeling as vulnerable as satin under the blade of a knife. He had shut himself away from her again; she could feel it.

"I don't," he said flatly. "Erica, look at your hands." She looked. Of necessity, the nails were short, unpolished. At the moment, the skin seemed to be at its worst, after a solid week of working with varnish and turpentine. She could tolerate gloves for only so long.

"You've been working like a slave. That's going to stop," he said harshly. "I couldn't do anything before..." He raked his hand through his hair, his head flung back, and for a second his eyes closed. When they opened again, they focused so intensely on hers that she felt frozen. "There's no going back to the way we were in Florida, Erica. You know that, don't you?"

She felt the color leave her face. The way they were in Florida? When he had invited her to take his love for her for granted, she had never doubted that love. Now she was beginning to feel there was nothing she could be sure of.

His voice grated like sandpaper against the grain, reacting to her silence. "I can imagine what you're thinking. The swimming pool—that was a stupid thing for me to say, Erica; you haven't a materialistic bone in your body. I know that. But you grew up in a certain environment... any child in your family had a choice of Yale or Harvard; financial security was an automatic given in life; fine paintings, sterling... *beauty* is what you grew up to. A *safeness* no one can understand as much as I can..."

"Those things mattered to me. I can't deny it," she said warily. The midday sun glared down on her strawberry-blond hair. The heat seared, odd hot beams that prickled her skin, seemed to deplete her energy. She didn't know how to convince him of anything. "Yet not as much as I thought they did," she said finally. "Kyle, I like it here—"

"I know you do. For now."

"For more than now. Safety isn't money, Kyle. *You're* the one who's working like a slave. You're going to drive yourself into the ground if you keep on this way..." Her voice faltered; she was aware that she was making no headway. Aware that they'd begun the whole con-

versation with his asking for her support for something
he believed he needed to do.

Confused, her mind stepped back five paces. Suddenly, nothing was simple. She loved his idea for the
new building, and they were bursting the seams of the
old shop as it was. Hold the man back? Never. And as
far as fear of the actual venture in terms of security—
no, just as she had never felt any fear at their change in
financial circumstances. Shock, yes; fear, no. In a world
of famine, she knew Kyle would find the last loaf of
bread, and give her the larger portion. And if he thought
the expansion a good business proposition, she knew it
was.

Unconsciously, they'd both fallen in step together,
walking back toward the shop. "Kyle?" They were about
to veer in different directions, and she didn't know how
to stop it. He turned at the insistence in her tone. "We
haven't argued in a long time," she said softly.

"Honey..." He sighed, though none of the stiffness
left his features.

"I don't want to argue with you. I'm *with* you, Kyle,
if you're sure taking on more is what you want to do
right now. I love your ideas..."

They stood facing each other. He placed a kiss on the
tip of her nose, his fingertips lingering on her cheeks.
"Prove it, then," he whispered. "Play hooky for the afternoon. Forget all about working completely, Erica..."

She cocked her head. "I'll need a bribe."

The kiss sustained her as she walked back to the house
and into the kitchen. But her euphoria didn't last. As she
mixed a batch of cookie batter, flour mixed with sugar
mixed with butter mixed with an occasional salt tear.
Stupid, the tears. She was furious with herself. Everything was *fine*. They were nearly out of debt, headed for
bigger and better things. She loved it here, no matter
what Kyle thought. And he wanted to be here. So what
was wrong?

The same thing that had been wrong for months, she

admitted to herself unhappily. Kyle had gone to the bank by himself, without consulting her, on a decision that affected both of them. He had always done that, made all the decisions, assumed a protective role.

And before Joel's death, she had always loved the niche he'd created for her in his life; she couldn't deny it. It had always been enough just to be Kyle's softness and laughter, his lighter side, his love. But it was not enough now. Her man was burdened with trouble he couldn't share with her, determined to shelter a lady who didn't want sheltering any longer. Having stood in his shadow for so long, it was a tenuous business trying to assert herself. The bookshelves were full of theoretical ideas; finding a solution was not so easy in real life, though. Kyle had never accepted help from anyone, always making his own way. He was the original strong, silent type . . .

And when she had offered help in this time of crisis, he had rejected her offering. She felt like a burden, not a mate, and was terribly afraid he saw her precisely that way. She had insisted on handling the antiques, loving that work anyway, but also knowing they had never really made a dent in Joel's debts. Kyle had done it all, taken on all the responsibility.

She didn't want to *be* a responsibility. She saw so many things more clearly now. How could a man really love someone he couldn't talk to without reserve, someone he couldn't share all his problems with? Someone who couldn't carry her own weight? And if he didn't love her as he once had; if he saw her as a responsibility; if he was taking on the expansion solely because he thought he had to for her sake . . .

Erica put the sheet of cookies in the oven and set the timer. Lord knew what they were going to taste like. When one started from scratch, the outcome could never be guaranteed. Wait and see, she told herself.

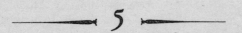

5

THERE WAS A war going on in the skies this late July afternoon. A simple sun-and-cloud war. One minute the clouds were allied in big, fat gray bunches, threatening a furious deluge of rain, and the next minute the sun attacked with such searing intensity that not a soul on the place had a shirt on—barring Erica.

She watched the skies with amusement, her hands on her hips. In a cream-colored gauzy blouse that loosely dipped to a V at her throat, and with her hair swirled into a careless coil on top of her head, she looked fresh and feminine in spite of the sultry day, with a graceful softness to her features. It had been one of those I'm-going-to-live-forever kind of days. In spite of her newly discovered affinity for varnish and brush, it had been a delight to get away from her work. She had taken an overnight trip to Milwaukee, and included in the packages still unwrapped in the house was a negligee designed to incite the most stoic man and a casual hostess dress in sunset colors. Kyle had stuffed a handful of bills in her purse, and told her not to come home until she was broke.

She was.

With the new building going up, the place had turned into a madhouse. Her two-day excursion had not really been for buying clothes, but for coming up with display ideas, and her car was still packed with the basics for the showroom—once the structure was done.

Her hazel eyes focused on the unfinished building. Though it was still bare boards at this stage, the sweet, lingering smell of new wood reached out to Erica like the smell of anticipation. The size and scope of the skeleton building were already there. In only two days, the workmen had made incredible progress. The building crew consisted of a half-dozen teenagers from the neighborhood whom Kyle had hired, Kyle, and yes, Morgan... who, to her amazement, could actually put in a full day's manual work.

Through the steady hammering and sawing, Kyle hadn't noticed her yet. His tanned back had a sheen of moisture to it, like baby oil, the ripple of muscle all the more pronounced because he was so lean, all sinew. As always in windy weather, his black hair curled, a phenomenon he hated like absolute hell. Watching him rake an impatient hand through the silky strands evoked another unconsciously sensual smile from Erica. His carpenter's apron was strung from low-slung jeans, the weight of nails and tape measures and tools drawing the jeans down, baring his navel in front and the last taper of spine in back. He radiated energy and purpose from every pore; she could feel the vibrations from a hundred yards away.

It was nearing quitting time. The men would stop at three; Kyle had other responsibilities besides the new building. Her glance flickered to Morgan, drawn by his easy burst of laughter at something one of the boys had said. Morgan... She still didn't quite understand why he was here. He had called one day; she had told him enthusiastically about the new building. The next thing she knew, he had shown up with a trailer in tow to camp in, prepared to take a three-week vacation to help them

out. His last vacation had been to Corfu; the one before
that to Bermuda . . . Manual work was not exactly his
style, but loyalty in friendship certainly appeared to be.

To be absolutely honest, she'd been slightly taken
back at the prospect of having Morgan underfoot for a
solid three weeks, but that was an unfair reaction and
she'd hidden it. Kyle needed the help, though he would
never have admitted it.

And Kyle . . . Things were still not perfect between
them, but the vibrancy was back in his body, his eyes,
as if he were alive again. Only occasionally did she catch
him watching her; at times she had the odd sensation
that he was treating her like spun glass . . . the way he
had delighted in weaning her from her antiques and turpentine for the trip to Milwaukee, the way he had insisted
she have some "mad money" to spend, the way he still
withdrew into himself too often. It was not right-side up
again, not all of it, but the world *had* tilted upward with
the project, and it was a far cry from being completely
upside down . . .

"Erica!"

She pivoted toward Morgan's voice. He was shouting
from a scaffold, his eyes welcoming even from the distance. She waved a vigorous hello over the noise, seeing
Kyle's head whip around in sudden awareness. Kyle
moved the moment he saw her, detaching the apron from
his belt loops as he shouted something to the others, then
leaping down from his perch and striding toward her.

She could feel anticipation surge through her bloodstream like white-water rapids; her color was high when
he kissed her in front of all the watching eyes. Her eyes
searched his, just for a moment, checking for those disquieting undercurrents that too frequently were a part of
his mood. Not this time. She could not doubt the sincerity
of his welcome, and she hugged him with a radiant smile,
loving the slippery warmth of his bare skin.

"So how'd it go?" he demanded, holding her at arm's
length to study her in turn.

"It went terrific! I have so many things to tell you—"

"In a minute." He kissed her again, full and hard, his bare chest pressing against her softer curves. When he came up for air, he studied the tremor of her soft lips and the revealing darkness in her hazel eyes. He glanced toward the men and immediately curved an arm around her shoulder, herding her in the opposite direction from them. "Erica, I don't even want to know how it went. That is the *last* overnight trip you're going on without me, lady."

Kyle pushed her into the passenger seat of the car. He slammed the door on her side and burrowed into his pocket, for his car keys as he crossed to his own side.

She raised her eyebrows quizzically at his scowl. "It really did go fine," she assured him calmly as the car roared to life.

"It did *not* go fine. How the hell did you expect me to sleep when you weren't here?"

As feminine strategies went, that brief separation had obviously been an excellent idea. She buried a smile. "You were alone for over a month when your father was ill—"

"That was different. I knew exactly where you were and had a trail of people guaranteeing that nothing was going to happen to you. There are all kinds of idiots running around a city the size of Milwaukee. Pickpockets, rapists, men on the make—the sheets were cold on your side of the bed," he added abruptly, his tone severe...and his eyes full of sheer blue mischief. She burst out laughing.

"It's been hot. You should have appreciated cool sheets," she pointed out.

"Like hell!"

"The four pickpockets I ran into—they're all in the hospital now. Remember that self-defense course I took in college—"

"The one that successfully taught you to defend yourself against four-year-olds? Go on."

"The one rapist I ran into—well, I just lifted my skirt to show off my knees. You always did tell me I had funny-looking knees, but it was still a real blow to my ego to see him go running in the opposite direction..."

"Obviously, he had terrible taste in knees. What else?"

"There *was* the one man who tried to pick me up in a restaurant—a big, tall redhead," she said with relish. "Selling computers—"

"I knew damn well there was going to be something," Kyle growled. "In fact, I knew the minute you walked out the door that it was a mistake..."

She looked at him interestedly. "You know, your last life must have been in the Middle Ages. Locked-up towers for the virgins, chastity belts, and all that."

"Chastity belts? *You* I trust, pint-size. It's the rest of the world that kept me up last night. Now go on about the redhead," he ordered.

"Hmmm. Well, he was just getting to the point of being a nuisance when his wife showed up, and the three of us had dinner together. She had a face..." Erica shook her head descriptively. "It was kind of goatish, that's all I can say. Long in chin and nose with little eyes sort of set back. Tufty hair."

Kyle shot a grin at her, and fingered an imaginary whisker in acknowledgment of her catty remark.

"Well, she was. And the conversation was...well, there was never a dull moment. They had four kids, none of whom were with them. Evidently, they always go to these conventions together, spending their free time harassing unsuspecting travelers like me—by showing them pictures. They had approximately nine thousand photographs of everything from children trying to kill each other wrestling to how much wall the baby could splatter when it was fed prunes. It didn't like prunes, and the poor thing had a goat face just like its mother..." She paused, relishing Kyle's uninhibited laughter. "Where on earth are we going?"

"Just out," he said lazily. "Away. Where I can hear about your trip for at least ten minutes in total privacy." He glanced away from her, but she knew he meant Morgan. For all the help Morgan had been, and even with the trailer he had rented to sleep in so they wouldn't be crowded in their small A-frame, he was still there for meals and evenings. The men always seemed to find enough to talk about, but by the time Morgan left each night, they were both so exhausted... Still, Erica had Morgan to thank for some of the changes in Kyle. He had come a very long way to help; and she had tried to go just as long a distance to make him feel welcome and to show her appreciation. Three weeks was not forever... but perhaps long enough to give Morgan a taste for being part of a family, steer him away from loose living and the free-floating women he'd always had a penchant for.

Kyle stopped within ten minutes at a gas station, pulling around to the side.

"This is where you wanted to talk?" she asked incredulously.

"Honey. We've been on the road for ten minutes. I have never taken you anywhere when you didn't have to stop within the first ten minutes..." She could feel the color chasing up her cheeks; he chuckled. "If you don't want to stop..."

"Dammit."

Her weak kidneys were legend. His concern for her stay in the city had fallen on deaf ears; she was more than capable of handling any problem that might have come up, men or otherwise. Kyle really knew that, too, in spite of his teasing. Still, it momentarily irked her that Kyle had the ability to reduce her responsible twenty-eight-year-old self to a mortified child.

"Do you think you can last for another few minutes

now?" he asked blandly when she came back out and slid into the car beside him.

"And would you like peanut-butter sandwiches for the next four years?" she wondered aloud, just as blandly.

He snatched her closer as he drove, until the wind swirled her topknot loose and long strands of hair whispered against the bare skin of his shoulders. She didn't care where they were going. Her smile just wouldn't fade. It was as if they had stepped back in time, to before the troublesome months, when their laughter was easy and just being together was a delicious pleasure. She laid a hand on his thigh and the car weaved promptly to the other side of the road. She found herself laughing again, as hickories, elms, maples shot past on the country lanes. "I'll bet no girl was safe with you when you were a teenager," she accused mockingly.

"You certainly weren't."

"You never listened." She remembered the long speech she had made about morals and commitments and let's get to know each other first . . . She'd kept on talking right through the morning she awakened next to him in bed. Horrified. Except for Morgan, Kyle had had no equal as a man of many conquests. But where Morgan was concerned, even a much younger Erica had guessed intuitively that there was an ego involved, that he thought of women as notches on a belt. With Kyle, she had instinctively given trust and yet wondered if she was being foolish. Her suspicions were misplaced; he made it more than clear that she was the only woman who mattered to him. His aim was not to conquer or to add notches to his belt but to fill a physical and emotional need. From the beginning, and every time they were together.

He stopped the car in a wooded glen that bordered an immense field of wheat, waist-high for as far as the eye could see. The sun and the clouds were still waging their little war in the sky. The clouds were bunched up charcoal masses clotted with rain, and a whisper of a breeze stirred their promise, but the sun was still hot, still stronger in the battle for the moment.

Kyle stood outside the car looking up as she made her way to his side. The birds and squirrels, so noisy in the morning, were silent, as if all the animals were napping at this time in the afternoon. A soft rush of whispering leaves encouraged a sense of privacy. Kyle looked down at her and took her hand as they walked out of sight from the car and road, down an old farmer's path that was overgrown. She hadn't the least notion where they were.

He bent to whisper in her ear. "I think you have the same thing on your mind as I have, Mrs. McCrery. There isn't a soul for miles around."

"What exactly is it that you have on your mind?" she asked suspiciously, laughter golden in her eyes as she glanced at him.

He sank onto a grassy spot in the shadow of a gnarled old hickory, lying flat on his back with his knees up, and rooted out a long blade of grass to stick in his teeth, making a whistle of it. She shook her head ruefully at him, settling down beside him on her knees. *"First, as I said, I want to hear about this trip of yours. You're all but bubbling over!"*

She was. For a woman who had barely been able to balance a checkbook a short time ago, she was one sky-high bubble of happiness at discovering the satisfaction of real accomplishment. She talked for twenty minutes, churning out a dozen ideas on how she wanted to set up displays, on what she needed from Kyle in the way of carpentry work to accomplish it. The marketing was her arena; for the first time since they moved here, she felt like an equal partner, with a chance to help build the McCrery enterprise into something they could both be proud of. Advertising was an automatic spin-off of the display work. "We haven't even begun to touch the rich folks who vacation on Lake Michigan, and Madison's an affluent little city. We were talking about taking on do-it-yourselfers, Kyle . . . and I thought we could expand into crafts as well—quilts and crewelwork and needlepoint; they blend with wood and add depth and color to a display. If we could find a few local women who already..."

"You know," he interrupted finally, "I like that blouse." He fingered the gauzy material between two fingers, studying the fabric intently. "It gives the illusion that you can see it all, and then it doesn't keep the promise. Even when you were standing full in sunlight, the flesh underneath was just shadowy—you don't mind if I check it out in a little more detail? Keep talking," he urged her politely. "I knew damn well you'd have a gift for setting up a classy showroom, lady. You get full applause for every idea so far."

She tried, but she seemed to be having an increasing difficulty following the thread of her own conversation. He propelled her flat on her back. Her strawberry-blond hair fanned out on the mossy grass behind her, and her golden eyes began to laugh up at his. He was very professorlike, gravely verifying that there were shoulders and breasts and ribs within the gossamer fabric, not just shadowy promises. "I can't believe how far you've progressed on the building in just two days, Kyle. You're going to be done in another week, aren't you? Here I've been selfishly rambling on, and I never even asked you about things here—"

"I changed my mind," he said severely. "I don't like this blouse at all." He raised her up, ordered her to lift her arms above her head, slipped the creamy summer material over her head, and promptly allowed it to decorate a bush. "Now is there some reason we need this?" He pointed to the lacy bit of bra. "I can't think of a reason in hell..."

"What if someone comes by?" The demurral was halfhearted, and he knew it.

"I have every intention of keeping you covered, lady..."

His lips were so warm, so soft from the sun, the scent

of grass, the ripple of the light breeze, the perfume of the wheat so intoxicating. It seemed to Erica that their loving had never had so much sweetness, so much urgency, so much sheer uninhibited joy.

They were both laughing as they stood up to take off the rest of their clothes, but their exuberant laughter had faded to something soft and secret, like a sound only the two of them could hear. When the clothes were gone, there was a moment when neither made a move to touch the other. Kyle stood, allowing Erica's eyes to sweep over his tall, bronzed form without shyness, as his own gaze took in, savored, loved her smaller feminine frame.

No man has a more beautiful body than you do. Did you know that? Would you like me to shout it out . . . ?

Every inch, Erica. Lord, I want you. Just as you are, this very instant . . .

They spoke with their eyes. They spoke in the way their lips joined, the way they both felt an identical sensual rush when their bodies finally touched. His hard thighs were pressed against her softer ones; her breasts swelled and tightened against his warm chest, and his skin . . . such supple skin beneath her kneading hands, which slid from the breadth of his shoulders to his taut male buttocks. He warmed beneath her hands, responsive to her every touch.

His lips left hers to trail down to her throat, silk-soft kisses that made her heart skip beats, that seemed to drug her into the illusion that she had left the ground. She had. Rather than bending, he lifted her playfully to kiss where he wanted, so that his face was level with her throat and then her breasts as he lifted her high, higher. Her legs wrapped around his waist for balance, and a husky sound escaped from her throat, half joyful laughter and half a helpless little groan as his lips burrowed between her breasts, his strong arms arching her back to offer the full satin flesh to his mouth. He raised her higher yet, pressing a kiss to her navel and then lower, his cheek brushing in that soft, curly triangle as she felt the crazy sensation of being weightless, higher than life, higher than breath.

When her toes touched the mossy earth again, there was still no sensation of reality. The spirit of soaring was intensified by the look in his eyes, by that deep turquoise brightness that came with loving, compelling tenderness. In some vague way, she was aware they were no longer standing but kneeling, then lying together on the soft moss. Her senses inhaled the shudder of need that racked Kyle's whole body, the husky whispers of loving in her ears, the surge that encompassed both of them as limbs suddenly feverishly tangled with limbs, neither of them wanting to rush and both of them in such a desperate hurry...

"Kyle..."

"How I love to see you happy, Erica. I'm going to take you so high you'll never come down..." He arched over her supple form, covering her, his kiss drowning the moaning cry in her throat when he joined with her. She felt so much love in his giving...

When the rain started falling, it made no difference at all, the soft, warm drops falling on skin that was already slippery. The scents around them intensified as if to prove that they were in another world. She almost hurt from so much love, a bursting joy within her, so loud that the thunder seemed quiet. She touched the sun and then seemed to explode...

Still he held her, rocking her back and forth until her heart stopped hammering, until they could both breathe normally again.

"You're beautiful," he murmured.

She already felt that. He'd already told her, in the best way a man can tell a woman. She just looked at him. Rain was streaming down; his face was damp, his hair curling wildly—he was blinking the water from his eyes. There were bits of grass on his neck and shoulders and a near carpet of it on his back.

He helped her up and shook his head at both of them

as he took in her own appearance. "How the hell am I going to put you back together so we can be seen in public again?" he growled in mock irritation, almost having to shout above the sound of the storm. He glanced up at the skies. "We have to be crazy!"

He tried to brush the grass off her back but the task was hopeless; the grass stuck to his fingers and her skin. Her bra refused to snap for him; her blouse, now soaked, did not want to go back on. She knew her hair was a wet tangle of grass, yet all she could do was look at him, her laughter part of the joy inside that just would not let her come back down to earth. Her eyes were a rich, dark gold, that certain sheen of color reserved for only one man's cache of treasures.

6

MORGAN WAS WAITING for them.

The late afternoon remained stormy, and the lights in the house were on. Erica was still laughing, Kyle pushing her ahead of him to hustle both of them out of the rain, although it was obvious there was nothing to hurry for—they were both soaked, cold, and grass-stained. Erica was well aware that her hair was irretrievably matted and that her blouse was probably ruined with snags and blotches of green. She couldn't have cared less...

Morgan was standing rock-still when Kyle closed the door behind them, locking out a distant crash of thunder. The bright lights in the kitchen heralded the fact that it was past their normal dinner hour. Morgan had started the meal for them. So thoughtful of him...but when Erica glanced up, she saw Morgan's eyes narrowed on both of them, a grim expression on his face that startled her from their laughter.

It must have been obvious what they had been doing. She shivered unconsciously, feeling the unwanted heat of embarrassment in her cheeks even as she glanced at

61

Kyle. "We didn't mean to be late," she said in a rush. "We just went out for a little walk..."

"Yes, Erica," Morgan said mockingly. He winked lewdly at Kyle, and she felt a wave of sheer distaste. Kyle appeared to ignore the wink as he offered her first crack at the shower and poured himself a glass of brandy.

She took the stairs two at a time. In the bathroom, she quickly discarded her damp clothes and turned on the hot water in the shower until the room was steaming. The pelting hot water soothed away the chill, yet she could not rid herself so easily of the resentment and annoyance she felt toward Morgan. She reminded herself how much help he was giving Kyle as she stepped out of the shower and enfolded herself in a thick, bright towel. She reminded herself, too, how much she cared for him, what a good friend he was... but she so desperately wanted to be alone with Kyle tonight! Since the building project had started, they had had a chance to put things back together, to reestablish communication, but Morgan *always* seemed to be there. They had had to steal away from their own home this afternoon...

By the time Kyle mounted the stairs, Erica had the hair dryer on full blast, a warm terry-cloth jumpsuit covering every inch of her in burnt orange. He said nothing, not that she could have heard anything over the whine of the dryer. Not, for that matter, that she would have said anything about Morgan...

She had never complained about Morgan in the past. These days, she thought fleetingly as she applied blusher and lipstick, Morgan was Mr. Consideration, all warmth and affection. It had not been that way when she first met him, at a time when he and Kyle had shared both a house and a reputation that would have put wolves on the kitty-cat list. The way Morgan used to look at her, the knowing expression that she saw on his face every time Kyle wasn't looking.

Morgan's bedroom should have had a revolving door; he certainly had no right to judge anyone else, but actually it wasn't judgment she saw in his eyes—only a comprehension that had mortified her. He seemed to look at her and speculate about how it was with her and Kyle. She would have felt foolish telling Kyle of her unease around his best friend, and it wasn't as if she'd felt ashamed.

She wasn't ashamed. She was in love with Kyle, and if she worried constantly that it had all happened too fast and too powerfully, those thoughts never diminished her love. Kyle wasn't looking for a child, and she had grown up, learned to look Morgan in the eye, wearing her love like a shield and her pride in that love like a cloak.

With one last flick of the brush, she finished dressing and headed back downstairs determinedly. Morgan had a glass of brandy waiting for her. He was wearing a charcoal short-sleeved shirt and lighter gray pants, the image of a manual laborer instantly dissolved by the skill and costliness of his tailor. Their conversation was stilted as they finished the preparations for dinner and waited for Kyle.

As she sipped at the brandy, Erica noticed hollows of weariness beneath Morgan's eyes, and felt foolish for her uneasiness. Stop this, she scolded herself finally. Stop being so . . . silly. She found a smile for him, her real one, and the social graces to put him at ease. It occurred to her that he might not be comfortable in his position as a third wheel. She did not have to remind herself again how hard he had been working—and only because he cared about her and Kyle.

Yet her nerves prickled uneasily once more when Kyle came back down, his damp hair curling at the edges of his collar, his pale blue shirt heightening the color of his eyes. He refilled his brandy glass before he sat down at the table, and for a moment Erica was afraid the easy laughter was gone; there was a hint of brooding stillness in him when he glanced at Morgan.

Then it was gone, just that quickly. Morgan brought platters to the table with a flourish that announced a gourmet delight. It was impossible to tell what he would come up with when he was given free rein in the kitchen. Tonight the menu was Chinese—chicken, pea pods, and peppers in a tangy-sweet sauce, rice, and a salad she could guess Kyle's reaction to, with sprouts, fresh mushrooms, some sort of raw fish.

"It looks delicious," Erica hurriedly assured Morgan.

"When are you going home so I can have my cook back, Morgan?" Kyle questioned blandly.

Morgan only chuckled. "Listen, McCrery, you can't survive exclusively on meat and potatoes. I've been trying to expand your tastes ever since we were in school together."

"Don't buy that," Kyle told Erica. "When we roomed together, he volunteered to do the cooking if I'd do the general cleanup. If I'd known I was going to end up the sacrificial lamb as a result of that arrangement..." He shook his head. "I can remember the first 'flaming' dish he put on. Or put out, to be more accurate. The effect was wasted on his redhead of the moment. We ate smoke for a week."

Erica chuckled.

"You're out of your mind," Morgan informed him. "I get sole credit for the fact that you're alive today, McCrery. You were trying to survive on four hours' sleep and potato chips."

"The only time I was sick in four years was the day you tried out that Indian curry. You'd have thought we'd been drinking contaminated water."

"It wasn't *that* bad—"

"*You* were sicker than *I* was."

Erica relaxed, familiar with their baiting of each other. Thunder crashed outside, lightning streaked a flight of stairs in the sky. She got up to close the long curtains at the front windows. When she returned to the table, she picked up her fork again, only to hear an insistent scratching at the back door. She did her best to ignore it. Blessedly, neither of the men seemed to hear anything.

She was relieved to hear them bickering normally; at times lately, they seemed to have less and less in common with each other . . .

When her plate was empty, Erica got up as if her sole purpose were to set it on the counter. The counter, of course, was a stone's throw from the back door. The cat was inside before anyone could notice—if the creature had only had the sense *not* to leap directly for Kyle. Morgan burst out laughing.

Nuisance, she had named the animal, and truthfully the feline looked as good as she was ever going to look after all Erica's care. The cat was much fatter, her coat almost healthy-looking . . . But not now. Drenched, Nuisance resembled an oversized rat. Kyle glared down beneath the table, as the cat promptly wound itself damply around his legs.

"She likes you," Erica said lamely. "Kyle, I couldn't just leave her out in the rain."

She quickly set down a saucer of milk to divert the cat, but Nuisance was already roaring a thunderous purr on Kyle's now damp-stockinged feet. He glanced again under the table and gave a mock shudder of disgust for Morgan's benefit.

"Cheer up," Morgan advised. "They say you can at least temporarily ward off a woman's maternal urges if you get her a pet. I have a feeling you two wouldn't exactly appreciate a baby right now. A cat's a hell of a lot cheaper."

Something changed; Erica couldn't define it. Kyle leaned back lazily in his chair, eyes riveted on Morgan. "Why on earth would you have the feeling we wouldn't welcome a baby right now?"

Morgan shrugged. "Well, obviously, financially . . ."

Kyle shoved his half-full plate away from him, shaking his head mockingly at Morgan. "Sorry, Shane, but *one* baby wouldn't be any more problem than *one* cat, financially or in any other way," he said shortly, and gave another wry shake of his head at Nuisance, who was staring up at him adoringly. "Though Erica *would* have to find the mangiest feline in the whole country to take on. I *had* hoped she could keep her secret a little longer. I have a continual nightmare that, given the least encouragement, she'd have a dozen cats wandering all over the place."

"Of all the unjustified, exaggerated..." Erica sputtered indignantly.

"Now you *have* been known to go overboard when you get started on a cause," Kyle chided teasingly. "Particularly a lost cause..."

But she was watching, mesmerized, as his long arm reached down and his fingers lazily scratched the cat's neck. When she bent down for a better look, his hand whipped back up to the table, but she wasn't fooled. *"You've* been feeding her, too," she accused.

"Never! *A cat?*"

"I thought we were going through an awful lot of milk."

"Erica. I *hate* cats." But his hand was sneaking down again and Erica smiled broadly at her big, tough, brooding Irishman.

"So *that*'s why you haven't produced a little McCrery," Morgan interjected harshly. "You think she wouldn't want to stop at one."

Erica's head whipped around at his strangely abrasive tone. A tone that Kyle suddenly matched. "Still worrying about it, Morgan? You'll be a godfather, all in good time. You're the only one we know with enough money to be godfather to the brood Erica and I want."

"And I'm sure they'll all be black-haired, blue-eyed little Irishmen," Morgan said sarcastically.

"You can bet on it." Kyle smiled.

Erica could have turned water to ice cubes with her smile. The brood of children she wanted was news to her. The subject of a family seemed to have come out of nowhere, along with Morgan's hostility and Kyle's matching antagonism. Kyle had wanted her to himself in the beginning. He had made no secret of that, and it was exactly what she had wanted as well. He'd been a busy man, and she'd wanted every free minute she could have with him. Only for the last year and a half or so had her maternal urges become more insistent yearnings... but then his father had become ill. Children *were* important to her, but never as important as Kyle.

The men moved away from the table, went down to the living room, and Erica hurried to take care of the dishes. Morgan was as uneasy as a prowling cougar. Restlessly, he paced to the drapes and back to his chair; then he was up again to pour drinks for both men. Though they were talking about the progress of the building, Erica noted again a charged tension between the two men that never used to be there. She didn't know what to make of it, but she had the curious feeling that if she didn't get away from them, the whole brilliant happiness of the earlier afternoon was going to splinter like shattered glass.

She finished the last of the dishes, switched off the counter lights, and scooped up the cat as she paused by the stairs. "Excuse me, will you two?" They were oblivious to her. Nuisance curled to her neck, encouraged by the rain-silken curtain of her hair. Upstairs, Erica sank into the chair in her own special corner of the room, feeling a sudden weariness as she reached for the basket of crewel beside her. As she worked with her hands, she felt the tension inside her evaporate. The lamp made a soft halo all around her in the peaceful room. The cat nestled at her side, batting interestedly at the bright yarn as she worked.

The men's voices carried upstairs, but she paid no attention. Absently, she noticed that there were two packages still to be put away. She folded the negligee with care and shook out the dress before hanging it up, admiring both garments silently, crumpling the wrappings and tossing them in the wastebasket. The little noises blurred the sound of voices from below, until she sat down with her embroidery again.

"... We've known each other a long time, yet only once, Kyle, did you ever *really* talk about your father," Morgan was saying. "We were both drunk out of our minds, we had just sent a pair of twin blondes home. Do you remember?"

The cat's claws instinctively tightened on Erica's thigh when she stiffened. Kyle's quiet voice had the kind of timbre that carried.

"I remember our sophomore year as a time when we took on everything in three-month binges, from philosophy to social causes to drinking. Hardly a time to put much stock in anything either of us said."

"You said he was a failure. You were scared as hell of following in his footsteps. You washed floors to put yourself through school, waited tables, *anything*, McCrery, to make sure you had what you needed to get to the top—"

"My father wasn't a failure," Kyle replied curtly. "I thought that, yes. I thought a lot of asinine things when I was twenty. He refused to do what he didn't want to do, and he lived as he chose to live. I no longer call that being a failure; I respect him for it. Rising to the top to meet someone else's standards doesn't build self-respect, Morgan. You should know that. You've played the game on your father's heels; I played the game to get out from under *my* father's. The end is the same. What exactly do you think you have if you don't live by your own rules? What do you think of yourself when you look in the mirror in the morning?"

There was a tense silence. Unease settled like a hard lump in Erica's throat as the voices wafted to her with undercurrents she had never heard before. As she glanced at the embroidery frame in her lap, she saw that the stitches were haphazard, awry. She dropped it, unconsciously putting the cool fingers of one hand to her forehead and stroking the cat with the other hand.

"That's all very nice," Morgan drawled suddenly. "But the point is that you're here. A little country town in the middle of nowhere. A lot of trees and your business, and a drive-in movie on a Saturday night—more power to you, if that's what you want."

"Shane, why the hell don't you say what you want to say?" Kyle said wearily.

There was another silence. "For how long?" Morgan asked finally.

"I don't know."

"One year? Ten? The rest of your life?"

"I don't know." He spoke so quietly that Erica had to strain to make out the words. She stood up suddenly and folded her arms instinctively across her breasts in a protective gesture she couldn't explain.

"It's not right. You know it isn't."

"It's none of your business, Morgan."

"I wonder whether you even asked her ahead of time if she wanted to come here after your father died. She talks it up real well, McCrery, but I don't think you're so sure. I'll even bet that you didn't consult her before you borrowed from the bank for that building. Did you?" There was a short silence, and then Morgan barked out a laugh that sounded triumphant.

As quietly as possible, Erica closed the door on them. She felt a wave of nausea flood through her. She hated arguments. She had grown up in a houseful of them, although her parents claimed to have a happy marriage. It was just their way. Because of "their way," she had nightmares so terrible that her mother had taken her to a psychologist when she was eleven. He had sent her home after the first visit. A very bright girl, he had said, certainly not in the least emotionally unstable. She was simply oversensitive, at a difficult age. She would outgrow it.

She hadn't. She closed her eyes, hearing the muted sound of voices raised in anger, and then, shortly afterward, a door slammed. Morgan going to his trailer.

She didn't understand. Vaguely, she was aware that Morgan was trying to champion her. That thought brought about a massive sense of distress inside. She didn't need champions, didn't want one . . . but so much *more* than that she hadn't understood. They were sniping at each other, not at all like the friends they had always been. Yet Morgan had come here solely to help; Kyle had seen Morgan through crises so many times . . . It made no sense.

Nor did destroying a friendship of long standing because of a thirty-minute argument, no matter what the cause.

Erica headed downstairs. It was tomb-silent below. Kyle was standing next to the couch, amber liquid in the glass in his hand. When she approached his side, his eyes met hers, hooded blue, and he took a sip from the glass. He had retreated inside himself and was as different from her lover of the afternoon as the sun from the moon.

"I couldn't help hearing," she said hesitantly.

"I heard you close the door. You missed the best part."

She took a breath. "Kyle, I don't know what it was about, but it doesn't matter," she said carefully. "Morgan . . . maybe he shouldn't have brought up your father. Maybe it sounded as though he was questioning you, Kyle, but . . . surely you know that he's really always been jealous of you? No matter how much he has, he never seems to have the . . . inner strength that you have. He's always challenged you. He comes to show off his toys; he comes . . ."

"What a good defender you make for him," Kyle snapped. "As he does for you. A mutual admiration society."

The comment stung. "I wasn't trying to defend him," she said quietly. "I just don't want the two of you to destroy a friendship that's important to you. I know he came here to help you, but I still have the feeling that things are really the other way around—that Morgan needs something from you right now, Kyle—"

"That's my Erica," Kyle interrupted wearily. He emptied the contents of his glass in a long gulp and stared at her. "You *do* like underdogs, lady. The only problem is that I've never been willing to play that role. Not for anyone." He refilled his glass with straight scotch from the sideboard cabinet. "And you're as loyal as they come," he added broodingly. "You'd stick with me through thick and thin and never tell a soul it was tearing you into little pieces."

"What are you *talking* about?" she said unhappily. feeling awkward as she stood frozen to the spot.

"Loyalty, Erica. The difference between loyalty and love. You've dug in with me; I know exactly what that feels like. I've been there," Kyle said harshly.

She stared at him blankly. He made loyalty sound like something sick. Emotions clogged her throat, hearing him talk to her this way after the afternoon in the wheat field a few hours before. She could easily have told him why she had dug in with him, could have said love *and* loyalty, but she was suddenly achingly certain that he would throw her feelings back in her face. Confused, she tried to back up. "I don't know what this has to do with your argument with Morgan . . ."

"Don't you? Morgan's got it all, Erica. Security, wealth, the kind of position in life you have a right to." His eyes were like ice as he forced a drink into her hand; she took it and gulped. It would have spilled if she hadn't. Her hands were trembling.

"What Morgan has or is has nothing to do with us. He's *your* friend, Kyle." She hesitated. "God in heaven, if you don't want him here, why don't you send him away?"

Kyle's brooding eyes settled on her. "Do you want him to go?"

Erica hesitated, afraid anything she said would be wrong.

"You find that such a difficult question?"

"No." She flushed, adding awkwardly, "And no, I don't want to see him leave. Not right now." Not when the two of them were at odds; not when their separating in anger would destroy the friendship. Nor did she want to be responsible for severing the tie between the two men.

"I didn't think you did."

His sarcasm wounded her. She turned away, feeling how stilted her movements were, and bent to turn out the light between the two chairs, setting down her drink. The shading darkness was better. All she wanted was to go back upstairs before he could say any more...

Suddenly, he was behind her, his hands on her shoulders spinning her to face him, her chin uptilted as she was trying to gulp for air. His fingers closed around her upper arms as if he wanted to shake her.

"Please, Kyle," she protested.

"What the hell are you *thinking*, Erica?" A desperate frustration seemed to explode inside him. He was a stranger, a strong man with too many feelings she could barely understand pent up inside him. "You're shaking like a leaf; you think I don't know you can't stand the sound of raised voices? Lord, Erica, I'd never hurt you, but I've got to know what you're feeling. I have to know you have the courage to make a choice for yourself, even if it means hurting people. You've got to take a stand, *not* from loyalty but from what you genuinely feel, what you need in your life. There's no love when there's no free and open choice with it—do you understand?"

How could he expect her to understand anything when he was shouting at her? Confusion and fear pulsed through her; all circuits crisscrossed inside. Then the confusion cleared, and she was left with a very clear picture in her mind of their lovemaking that afternoon, of the rain falling on them and her own whimpered pleasure, of his laughter, his mastery of her, of the moment she had given every vestige of herself in loving him. The man towering above her, shouting at her, made a mockery of that. Her hand reached up and cracked like lightning across his cheek.

The blow must have stung like fire. His cheek was red, his eyes dulled with shock. She had never felt so deadly calm. "You wanted me to express how I was feeling?" she asked evenly. She nodded for him when he didn't answer. "Fine," she said flatly. "You got what you wanted, Kyle."

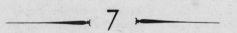

7

ERICA WOKE BEFORE the sunrise, to a scratchy little tongue trying to wend its way into her ear. Her hand automatically reached outside of the covers to stroke the cat. A thunderous purr resulted.

Unsmiling, she opened her eyes. The room was gray in the predawn light, lifeless and silent. She had locked the door to the loft; she had no idea where Kyle had slept.

The air was chilly, and a crisp breeze stirred the draperies at the open windows. The cat nuzzled insistently, uncaring of the early hour, the chill, anything so irrelevant as heartache. Nuisance wanted food, and to go back out on the prowl. In a few minutes, Erica was dressed in a short, loosely knit topaz top and dark brown jeans. She tried applying makeup to hide the shadows under her eyes, but the effect looked painted; she wiped it off, brushed her hair vigorously, and headed downstairs, the cat leading the way.

Kyle and Morgan were both in the kitchen nursing their coffee, their shoulders hunched and weary. The sun was peeking through the kitchen window; the men for the building project would be arriving soon. Kyle and Morgan were talking in low, morning voices, but she felt both pairs of eyes on her as she prepared a bowl of milk for the cat and then poured a cup of coffee for herself.

She felt Morgan. He radiated concern. She didn't want it.

Kyle looked . . . the problematic Celt he was. He had not brushed his black hair yet, and he had probably slept in his T-shirt, but he had the kind of good looks that were enhanced rather than obliterated by hollows beneath his eyes. He was straddling the stool, his jeans stretched taut over his lean thighs, all hard muscle and no waste. He had the look of a very strong and complicated man, who could wear his melancholy like an air of mystery, and whose dishevelment implied sensuality to her, even now.

The cat lapped up the milk. Erica found a breakfast roll for herself, and as soon as Nuisance was done drinking, she opened the back door and followed the cat outside.

"Erica?"

She heard Kyle's quick step, but she closed the door behind her quietly, deliberately. She wasn't giving him the silent treatment, nor was she sulking. She simply had nothing to say. What could she possibly say when he had all but told her he no longer loved her?

Her mind was still spinning webs of anger and hurt just as it had through the long night. It was not the kind of morning on which she noticed the crystal gleam of sunlight on dew-soaked grass, or the bright chatterings of cardinal and blue jay above her head as she walked toward the old shop. She just kept remembering the sting of her palm, the cold look in his eyes, the nauseating realization that her love and loyalty meant nothing to him . . .

Absently, she tossed the unfinished breakfast roll to

a trio of squirrels waiting hopefully at the edge of the woods. Kyle seemed to have been trying to tell her last night that it was over. There's no love without an active choice, he'd said.

But there *was* love without choice: the feeling a parent had for a child; the sensations one felt on seeing an attractive person of the opposite sex; the feeling one had when the sun was out on a certain kind of day. But the kind of love that mattered in a marriage was not free at all; it involved commitment, an *active* choice day after day, just to live through those days when the sun wasn't shining, the days after a spat over a good-looking man who had made a pass, the days when one of them had the flu and courtesy was the only thing that helped them get through the hours. One made that choice to muddle through because the love was worth it, because the relationship was worth it... because the man was worth it, she thought achingly. And she'd made her choice; it just increasingly seemed that Kyle was choosing differently.

Leave? she wondered wrenchingly. Was that what this was all about? Did he want her to leave? Toss away nine years of marriage... She couldn't. She just couldn't, no matter how he felt—or what he didn't feel for her any longer. Not this minute, not just like that, like the blind turn of a card...

What she needed, she told herself, was work. And the work was there, waiting for her in the shop. The new building was almost finished; very soon everything would have to be moved, which meant packing all the small items... There were bills to pay and invoices to make out, orders for materials to check through...

She sat at the ancient desk with her coffee cup and buried herself for almost two hours—succeeding, almost, in putting a share of her problems on hold until she felt better able to cope with them. Weary finally, she stood up and stretched, then wandered idly to the window.

Her eyes widened in surprise. A pickup was pulling
up outside the door, a decrepit old thing that had been
painted a shiny yellow and was decorated with decals
shaped like bright orange and green flowers. In the back
was a huge table secured with ropes. Beside it stood a
monster of a dog, woofing, his nose jutting out precar-
iously to catch every last vestige of wind on his dark,
furry face. In spite of herself, Erica managed a smile
and hurried outside.

"Hi there!" The speaker was a little sprite of a woman,
with brownish-gray curls fringing her forehead and snap-
ping gray eyes. Perhaps forty, the lady had the kind of
wrinkles on her face that said she'd never been as careful
about staying out of the sun as she should have been and
a smile that never did quit. "Down, you ornery old thing,
and stop all that barking!" she scolded the huge shaggy
dog, then turned to Erica. "I've got a problem I'm hoping
you can help me with. You're Kyle's wife, aren't you?"

Her step was as sprightly as the brilliant orange blouse
she wore, never minding the arm encased in a heavy
plaster cast. She offered her left hand for Erica to shake
instead of her right, which obviously couldn't do the job.
Her hand was warm and welcoming, her handshake firm.
"I'm Martha Calhoun; we're neighbors. Got a dairy farm
about five miles down the road. We were friends of Joel
McCrery's once upon a time. He used to stop for dinner
once a month and take us all at poker. All right, get
down," she shouted to the whining animal. "But don't
go scaring everyone all over the place!"

Erica blinked when the dog promptly vaulted over the
side of the pickup. "He's half horse?" she questioned
dryly.

The lady laughed. "He's half rabbit. Likes raw carrots.
Intimidates half the countryside with the look of him. I
never did know whom he belongs to, but he's got a thing
about riding in my truck. We call him Lurch."

"I can see why." The dog had a loping, crooked gait

as if his legs didn't quite know how to accommodate his size; he also had ears that flopped, the soft eyes of a spaniel, the tail of a setter, and the thick, soft coat of a St. Bernard.

"He's the stud of the neighborhood," Martha Calhoun said disgustedly. "If I were a female dog, I'd take one look at him and turn my nose in the air. But I know of four litters in the last two years, and one of the bitches was a prize English setter. Nancy Chase hasn't talked to me since."

Erica gathered that Nancy Chase owned the setter. The dog bounded close enough to sniff her, and she extended her palm for him to check out. The dog promptly washed her whole hand, sitting down next to her to do a most concentrated job of it.

"He doesn't like people," Martha offered sadly.

"I can see that."

Martha laughed, motioning to the bed of the daisy-yellow pickup. "I should have come over here to meet you before! Come and look, would you, while I tell you all about my aunt Beatrice."

With Lurch dogging her heels, Erica made her way to the back of the truck. The table was mahogany and had perhaps been intended to stand in someone's castle hall a century or so earlier. The legs were intricately carved, an "N" in an upholstered wreath dominating one drop leaf, a carved eagle on the other. At one time, the top must have been faced with leather, but sometime in the recent past it had simply been finished and varnished—and, unfortunately, all but destroyed. Huge whitish rings, apparently caused by potted plants, scarred the wood . . .

"I'm sure it's very valuable," Erica said tactfully.

"Very. The 'N' is for Napoleon. The period is Empire French, just so you can avoid it in the future. I covered it with plants so I wouldn't have to look at it, but now you can see what I've done."

Erica nodded with another glance at the water spots.

"It's all right," Martha said cheerfully. "Go ahead and say it."

"I never thought a table could actually look *pompous...*"

Martha laughed again. "But then, you've never met my aunt. And I got a letter from her this morning saying she'd be here in ten days from England—"

"So you've got ten days to get the table back in shape?" Erica viewed the piece with a critical eye. Finally, she shook her head. "I'd love to help you, honestly. But the antiques I've been working on have all been American, nothing this old or valuable. Kyle would know what to do, but he's so tied up—"

"Honey. *I* know what to do; it's this broken arm that won't let me do it. I can see you're not dressed for messy work at the moment, but..."

No, she wasn't; however, Martha's eyes were bright with pleading. Just seeing her gave Erica enormous pleasure. How long had it been since she'd chatted with another woman?

"We might not even have to refinish it," Martha coaxed. "Have you got a smoker around the house?"

"Smoker?" Erica asked blankly. "No..."

"Well, we need ashes."

Within an hour, Erica had found laughter she had never expected to find that morning. Ashes and lemon juice were what Martha had in mind for removing the water spots, spurning all the scientific preparations stored in Kyle's shop. While Erica changed her clothes, Martha made coffee for both of them. Then they discussed the ashes... and along the way, hair styles, clothes, living on a farm, cooking, and animals. Martha had a lively sense of humor, and by the time they headed back outside they were chattering like friends of long standing.

They shelved the lemon and ash mixture temporarily in favor of another old-fashioned preparation for removing water stains: vinegar and cold water. Erica sat in the bed of the truck, wearing a halter top and shorts, working there because the table was too heavy for them to lift down. Occasionally, she glanced up to the sound of hammering and sawing where the new building was going up. Lurch was lying in the middle of the fray, being stepped over frequently, completely oblivious.

"He's unbudgeable," Martha said ruefully. "I should have left him home. And I never meant to take up your whole morning—"

"No problem," Erica assured her. She added absently, "The vinegar's good, but not good enough."

"I've heard a little alcohol on a fingertip rubbed really hard—"

Finally, they gathered paper and a small stack of twigs and crouched over them in the driveway, Erica waving her hands furiously to get the fire going. "This is ridiculous," she said idly.

Martha agreed.

"No one would go to this much trouble to get a few tablespoons of ashes. Anyone who saw us would be looking for straitjackets on sale."

Martha agreed.

The ashes were cooled and collected. Martha's broken arm in no way inhibited her ability to make trip after trip to the kitchen. She fetched more vinegar and water to remove the old furniture polish; then iodine to hide the tiny scratches; then lemon juice to blend with the ashes for removing the water spots. The mixture worked, although Martha had an alternative potion in mind—toothpaste mixed with baking soda.

Erica laughed harder each time Martha brought back something else from the house. "Where did you ever *hear* of all these home remedies?"

"Oh, in any old farming family this kind of lore is handed down from generation to generation. Needs must, as they say. A long time ago, the woman of the house didn't have a store to pop to every time she needed something. I just wish I could do the work myself; I've ended up taking your whole morning. If it were only my *left* arm that was out of commission—"

"What on *earth* is going on?"

Morgan had crept up behind Erica and pressed a kiss on the nape of her neck. The two women had been so immersed in the project that neither of them had heard him approach. Morgan's hand lingered on Erica's shoulder as he surveyed the table—and the half of her kitchen that seemed to be on the truck bed, from bowls to spoons to the crazy mix of household supplies.

"This is Morgan Shane, Martha," Erica said. "Martha Calhoun—she's a neighbor of ours, Morgan."

"I take it that's your dog in the middle of the sawdust," Morgan guessed dryly. There was charm in his smile for Martha, but his eyes rested on Erica, an intent look at her clinging halter top and the long stretch of midriff below it. "I've got to get back to it. Just wanted to tell you I'd be going into town for lunch . . . and I wanted to see how you were faring this morning." One finger tapped her cheek, and Erica felt a spark of warmth because Morgan had checked on her, a reminder that he had braved an argument out of worry over her the night before.

Then he was gone, with a wave and a good-bye for Martha, who stared after him with wide-eyed interest. "I'll have to ask Leonard," she said gravely, "but that hunk can put his slippers under my bed anytime."

Erica burst out laughing. She had already formed a very definite impression of Leonard and the kind of life the Calhouns had together. Their dairy herd consisted of sixty cows, just short of good size, according to Martha. They were up at three every morning to be ready to milk at five, and the second milking didn't end until eleven at night. That left only a few hours' sleep every night, so a nap was essential every day for both of them. It was the kind of life that took closeness between couples for granted. Without it they couldn't have survived.

The Calhouns had a teenage son whom Martha dismally labeled immature, and whose sole interest in life, it seemed, was playing drums. Their seven-year-old daughter already needed braces and apparently lived in trees. Martha spent her time alternately worrying that the girl was going to kill herself climbing, or that one or all of them would go deaf from the constant drum practice. Erica pictured Leonard as stocky and steady, probably no better-looking than Martha but just as good-humored. He *had* to be, in a house where shaving cream was mixed with food coloring to make finger paints, and toothpaste was used to clean pewter. That Martha was happily married was as obvious as her clear, bright eyes and her smile that never took a rest.

"We aren't going to have to strip the finish off this, you know," she said with satisfaction. "We'll just use a good, strong coverup polish..."

The table was nearly done, the water spots barely perceptible, the scratches hidden. Kyle, a perfectionist, would never have allowed it to leave his shop without refinishing it, but Martha claimed it looked a lot better now than it did when she first got it, which was more than the monstrosity deserved.

"Don't tell me you've got a recipe for polish, too," Erica pleaded teasingly.

"A third of a cup each of boiled linseed oil, turpentine, and vinegar. Preferably cider vinegar. For the curves, you use a soft old toothbrush and brush it on real lightly." She waved Erica back as she started to leap down from the truck. "Hold on! I'll get it. I told you, it's the least I can do after you've dropped everything to take care of me."

"I've enjoyed it," Erica admitted truthfully, but in the back of her mind was her gratitude for these few hours of no heartache.

"You're coming for dinner tonight," Martha insisted. "The only thing I *can* do with my left hand is cook. Don't bother saying no. Leonard will *never* believe I've found someone who likes Lurch!" She was back in ten minutes, her makeshift polish in a well-shaken jar. "Kyle must have changed since he was a boy," she said absently.

"Pardon?" Erica whirled so quickly that she almost upset the jar. Martha's words had penetrated the numbness she'd shrouded herself in all morning.

"Your husband," Martha said wryly. "Now, *mine* wouldn't hurt a fly, but if any man as good-looking as that brown-eyed blond kissed me, he'd have been in traction before he got out the door."

"Morgan?" Erica said incredulously, and chuckled. "Martha, that's just his way. He's been Kyle's friend for years."

"That's funny. I could see right off *we* were going to be friends, and I haven't had urge one to kiss you," Martha pointed out blandly.

Erica shook her head with a grin. "Morgan's just like that," she repeated, and then hesitated, polishing the wood with long, careful strokes. "Kyle and I hit a little rough spot," she confided after moment's thought. "Morgan was the first one to offer help. There really aren't many friends like him." Martha was silent, and Erica glanced at her. *"Really!"* she insisted. "He really is!"

"Evidently, he is—to you," Martha agreed smoothly. "As I said, Kyle must have changed."

Martha had ten years on Kyle. At eighteen, she had been Martha O'Flaherty when Joel McCrery was an occasional visitor to the O'Flaherty household, and she'd served on occasion as Kyle's baby-sitter.

"Oh, I regretted it," Martha said ruefully. "Kyle accepted no one's rule, denied that he ever needed anyone to take care of him. So he'd take off and disappear until his father came back, worrying everyone sick. And if *anyone* dared criticize anything Joel McCrery did..." Martha shook her head expressively. "Nine years old and one time he took on a grown man who said Joel could have spent a penny's more time on work and a penny less on Irish whisky. This was a smaller community then, and we all rather thought Joel was digging a hole for himself and dragging his son in with him, but for the most part we kept quiet. Maybe we were wrong. Everyone liked Joel; he just wasn't a simple man... His wife died when Kyle was real young, and Joel was never the same after that. We all tried, but Kyle was the only one he cared for... And Kyle, he turned out fine once he stopped being a perfect little hellion. You're trying to rub the finish off?" she questioned Erica curiously.

Erica looked at her hands, white-knuckled from the thorough polishing she was giving the wood. Martha was talking about loyalty in the way Kyle had related to his father, and *loyalty* was a word Kyle had treated with contempt and disparagement the night before. Digging a hole and dragging his son in struck another painful spot; if Kyle was in a hole, it was Erica's nature to dig in with him, as if she couldn't help herself.

She felt as if Martha had inadvertently provided the missing puzzle pieces with her casual comments. Troubled, she felt she finally had caught a glimpse of something that really mattered, that would really help her understand Kyle... but she could not put all the pieces together. She ached when she thought of Kyle as a child. Joel sounded irresponsible, Kyle as if he had far too much to handle for one little boy. Fiercely loyal... independent, needing no one... Those traits were all echoed in the mature Kyle. She thought fleetingly of an earlier conversation she'd had with him, when he'd seemed to feel guilty for not loving his father as he felt he should have... yet how could he? How much could anyone put on one little boy before he started feeling resentful? Before love changed to a sense of duty? But what did any of it have to do with their marriage?

"...class president," Martha continued irrepressibly. "But he *did* have a reputation with the girls. Hell on wheels, I believe, is the polite phrase. Always knew he would never settle for a small-town girl like the ones he took out, though. In fact, I would have guessed you for Kyle's wife just by the look of you."

"What on earth do you mean by that?" Erica asked, surprised. The table was completely finished, shining under the midday sun. There were a half-dozen bowls and various other items to put away, but . . .

"Oh, I can picture pretty well how you'd look if you were all dressed up. High class right down to the toenails, an aristocratic nose, silks and emeralds . . ."

Erica chuckled, with a pointed glance at her shorts and halter, well splashed by this time, her knees red from kneeling. "I see what you mean," she said, deadpan.

"Oh, it's there," Martha insisted. "Believe it or not, it's there, even dressed as you are. Thank God the personality doesn't fit. From the time I was a teenager, I had a picture in my mind of the sort of girl Kyle would marry. She certainly wasn't the kind to let a mutt jump all over her or get down on her hands and knees the way you have all morning. I figured her for a real beauty but a sheltered type; he was always so protective. Anyway . . ." Martha pivoted around, her hand screening the sun from her eyes, searching for the dog. She turned with a smile for Erica, who had both arms full of supplies to take back to the house. "I'll see you—say, about six tonight? Bring Kyle, of course, if you can tear him away from the work." She chuckled, adding, "Watch this."

The hammering and sawing had stopped as the lunch hour approached. Lurch was lying on a pile of boards, surrounded by tools and half covered in sawdust, his head drooping in sleep. Martha called to him, but the dog didn't even raise an eyelid. She marched to the truck, got in, and started the engine, with another grin for Erica. Lurch sprang up instantly at the sound of the truck engine, and galloped past Erica in a blur of parti-colored fur. When the truck pulled out of the yard, the dog was settled in the back with his head angled out to catch the wind.

8

ERICA'S SMILE SLOWLY faded as Martha's pickup pulled out of sight. Balancing the assorted pails and buckets, she glanced toward the house. She knew Kyle was inside; it was lunchtime. She was going to have to face him and talk to him for the first time since last night, and she hadn't the least notion of what she was going to say.

Her feet obligingly picked up and moved, but she was conscious of her disheveled hair, the skimpy halter top and shorts. Hardly the window-dressing sort of wife Martha had her figured for. The kind Kyle wanted? Her step faltered again at the door, weighted down by a frightening feeling of hopelessness. She'd learned a great deal about Kyle from Martha, but not enough to erase the feelings of frustration and hurt left by their argument, the memory of Kyle's face when he had shouted at her . . . The bowls clattered in her arms and she raised her chin, her bleak eyes turning tawny in resolve.

As an entrance, it lacked something. Pushing the back door open with her hip, she hurried to the counter before half the clutter in her arms gave way entirely. The tiny iodine bottle managed to slip to the floor and roll around, barely noticed as she dropped the rest helter-skelter on the counter.

Kyle was sitting at the table; from the corner of her eye she saw an empty plate in front of him, and another plate with a sandwich obviously intended for her. She saw as well that he wore jeans and boots, that his bare chest and back were burnished from yet another morning in the sun... His light blue eyes silently caught hers.

She bent down to snatch up the iodine bottle, averting her eyes, thoroughly irritated. He was smiling, obviously amused at the chaotic mess of toothpaste and vinegar, iodine and ash... among other things. She had laughed at the same thing all morning... but she felt too tense now to smile, and she resented his mirth. At that moment, she resented everything about Kyle. The smooth slope of his shoulders was pure gold, as if his skin still held the warmth of the sun. She felt an annoying urge to touch him, to change the quiet, watchful blue in his eyes to the fire of turquoise she saw when she was in his embrace; she felt an overpowering urge to hold on and be held in a way that would erase the memory of his hurtful words. It wouldn't do. To reach out after he had wounded her so badly would show a lack of pride, and Erica's expression remained distant, radiating the aristocratic cool Martha had talked about.

Kyle cleared his throat. "Erica. Last night..."

"Let's leave it," she said swiftly. The put-away jobs were all done, and she seemed to have little choice but to sit across from him and pick up the sandwich.

"I was angry," he said quietly. "But not at you, Erica. I never meant to take it out on you—"

"I met someone this morning," she remarked. "A woman named Martha Calhoun. You used to know her, I understand? She asked us for dinner tonight."

"Erica—"

"You don't *have* to go; I can fix something for you and Morgan ahead of time. But I think *I* will. I liked her very much..."

There was a short silence, while Kyle studied her averted face and nervous movements. The thing was, she was terribly afraid she was going to cry if he pressed the subject of last night's argument. She didn't want to hear again what he thought of her love or her loyalty. It was hard enough trying to assimilate that she was sitting across from Kyle and yet their marriage was disintegrating, that for some impossible reason the sandwich was even going down and she had actually laughed that morning, that nothing seemed to alter the physical awareness of him she had always had. When his hand reached over to cover hers, she could no more have pulled away from him than she could have stopped breathing.

"We'll go to dinner at Martha's," he said softly. "Maybe later you'll feel like talking."

"You don't have to go if you don't want to."

He ignored that. "Erica, I think we've both had more stress than we can handle lately. The roof's going up tomorrow; that should take three days, more or less. After that, there's electricity and all the trimmings, but we should be able to steal a few days... Erica, I want a few days alone with you."

He went on, his tone strangely soothing. She had the ridiculous sensation that he was trying to calm her, and she resented that, too. He had always known her too well, had always been the only person in her life who knew exactly how to gentle her out of her resentment. She listened vaguely. Perhaps they would go to the Door Peninsula, he was saying, drive along the shore of Lake Michigan... see some treasures, lost ships, the lighthouse at Vermillion, perhaps do some diving...

Shortly after that he got up, bent over to place a kiss on the sun-streaked crown of her head, and went back out to work.

"A dairy farm?" Morgan said incredulously, and then laughed, hooking an arm around Erica's shoulder as he walked her outside. Kyle was still upstairs, taking a quick shower. "Are you going to have to churn your own butter for dinner?" Morgan asked blandly.

"I think they might be a wee bit more automated than that in this day and age," Erica said dryly. "And before you even ask, no, I won't be required to put on a big white apron and sit down with a pail to get milk for the meal."

Morgan's eyebrows shot up. "I was never going to ask that."

"No?"

"I was just going to remind you again that I've got chops and a grill and an unopened bottle of Chivas. Just because Kyle's hung up on the country scene doesn't mean you couldn't stay here with me. Or is Kyle so possessive he doesn't let you off the leash?"

"Woof."

Morgan looked appropriately disgusted, and Erica whirled when she heard the screen door slam behind her. Kyle strode toward her, dressed as casually as she was; both had opted for off-white pants and dark brown tops. The blend of colors accented Kyle's bronzed skin as much as it showed off her own red-blond coloring.

"Trying to beat my time again, Shane?" Before she'd had a chance to say word one, Kyle had handed her into the car.

"A losing battle," Morgan complained.

"But then, I've told you that before. Don't drink all the Chivas."

Erica sat back in the seat as he started the car, feeling as vulnerable as violets, her emotions short-circuiting all rational thought as she brooded over their unresolved quarrel. An afternoon of work seemed to have solved nothing, and the hurt simply didn't want to fade. She had never before in her life been so distraught as to strike anyone. And to do that to Kyle, whom she loved more than anyone . . .

"I'm trading buckets of roses for frowns this evening," he murmured next to her.

"Pardon?"

Those blue eyes seared into hers just for a few seconds as he put the car in gear. "I don't want you to think I'm trying to coax you into a happier mood, sweet, but you look somewhere between delectable and delicious."

"I'm wearing tennis shoes," she said flatly. "Martha's suggested attire."

"I can't help that."

"Kyle—"

"We're not going to argue now. We'll talk when we get home. And in the meantime, whether you like hearing it or not, you look very special; you smell very special; and Martha's a crazy enough lady that you just might even have a special time." He held up a hand. "Truce?"

She took his hand, touching fingertips to fingertips. His hand folded around hers, and she averted her eyes, staring out the window. She knew he hadn't forgotten the quarrel, either; his light humor was tentative, as gentle as the touch of his hand, and just as grave as the hidden light behind his eyes.

"What are you thinking of now?"

Dammit. Did he have to catch every frown? "Morgan can be extremely exasperating on occasion," she said lightly.

His hand shifted to the steering wheel. "Such as?"

"He doesn't understand the difference between being protective and being possessive. He's always teasing . . ." She shrugged lightly. "Sometimes it's funny. Sometimes I think he deliberately misunderstands."

"What exactly, Erica?"

She propped her feet against the dash and leaned back. "Nothing. Really. He just made this joke about your being possessive and my being on a leash. It didn't strike me as funny. But then you're not that way, thank God. You never have been. You're protective, but you've never had a macho attitude of you *can* do this, you *can't* do that. Possessive. Overpossessive. Chauvinistic. Domineering—"

"I get your drift," Kyle said dryly. His hands tightened on the steering wheel. "Love doesn't work on a leash. Unfortunately."

"Unfortunately?"

"Trust, honey. It's like a silken thread that sometimes has to be as strong as steel. Why," he suggested lightly, "don't you tell Morgan to go straight to hell?"

She shook her head, grinning. "He needs saving too badly. I've got to turn his attitude around before he takes on another redhead."

"And breaks her heart."

"And breaks her heart," Erica agreed.

Kyle pulled into the Calhouns' drive. "He's damned good at that, Erica." He wasn't smiling.

She puzzled over the look on his face for an instant, and then gave up trying to interpret it. Martha came flying from the house like a miniature bombshell, all bright colors and waving hands and huge smile.

"Darn it! Do you believe I invited you at milking time? And I haven't even started dinner! Unforgivable. Leonard told me I was a disgrace."

Kyle denied that. When they emerged from the car, Erica got a hug first, and then Kyle, who kept his hand affectionately on Martha's shoulder, assuring her that she was not a disgrace but the same scatter-brained, appealing nitwit he'd always known. Erica started smiling in spite of herself and didn't stop. Martha told him he was probably the same bullheaded, stubborn idiot he'd always been, but at least he had a minor claim to good looks. Kyle told her she didn't have that problem, but she was undoubtedly as bossy as ever.

The talk went on as they passed through the house to get Kyle a beer. The house was just like Martha, bright and cluttered and busy. Erica could hear the sound of drums coming from a nearby barn, to which their son had obviously defected. Leonard appeared, as soft-eyed and gentle a man as Erica had expected. He ignored

Martha and Kyle and took Erica's hand. Would she like to see the dairy equipment?

She would. Having no concept at all of a contemporary dairy farm, she was curious as she followed him from place to place. The cows were kept in stalls so clean they gleamed like a Cadillac's chrome. Nothing so unsterile as a human hand intervened in the process of getting milk from the cow to the consumer. From the animal, the milk was pumped through long, gleaming tubes to another room that held storage tanks. Trucks came three times a week to make pickups. The cows were huge, big-eyed, and gentle. Waddling around their feet were ducklings, which had free run of the yard. There were also pecking chickens, a pair of dogs, and a variety of cats, all colors.

"You mean my milk is actually three weeks old by the time I get it from the grocery store?" Erica demanded unhappily.

"At least. With almost all of the vitamins pumped out of it by that time. When you taste the milk at dinner..."

Dinner was the problem, Kyle told her. Martha was willing to make an effort at it, but in the interim the Calhouns' seven-year-old was discovered to be missing. The McCrerys were invited to solve the tougher of the two problems.

It was crazy. The entire evening was crazy. All Erica could think of was the thousand dinner parties remembered from a childhood when it was considered a mortal sin to pick up the wrong fork.

In contrast, tonight Kyle spent ten minutes arguing about the international implications of a drop in the Dow Jones average as he and Leonard drank beer. Erica fed a baby rabbit with a bottle. Martha chattered as she strewed out feed to the chickens, then fixed fresh water bottles for the rest of the animals, all of which made an incredible racket at feeding time. The Calhoun boy kept playing his drums. At first he seemed to favor contemporary rock, then went back to the Beatles, then to old-time jazz.

Martha whisked the rabbit out of Erica's hands, then ordered her to go with Kyle and stop worrying about helping with dinner. No one thought her capable of organizing anything, Martha complained, when in fact she was quite brilliant at it. Leonard begged to differ. She'd broken her arm tripping over even ground. Martha could remember a time he'd thrown out his back picking up a nickel off the floor.

Erica felt a large palm nudging at the small of her back, and she walked with Kyle back outside, past the barns. "Are they always like that?" she asked with a grin.

"I haven't any idea. Leonard was probably sane before he married her." His smile matched her own. "This was originally Martha's family's farm. When I was a kid, I thought it was the richest place on earth."

"It is," she agreed. In love and laughter. She was only beginning to understand that Kyle had been short-changed on these things as a child. The way Martha had whipped her arms around him and hugged . . . Erica had the unaccountable impression that Martha was still seeing a lonely, sensitive, stubborn little boy with too much pride, totally overwhelmed by the effusive O'Flaherty clan. Erica saw, too, that Martha loved to bully him with love, that she was delighted Kyle had turned out strong and handsome, and not quite so difficult to bully. The thought made her smile, even as she felt a lingering sadness, thinking of Kyle as a child, then of their quarrel the night before.

"Where exactly are we going?" she asked idly. They had crossed out of the farmyard and were striding along a farmer's path bordering a field of wheat.

"There's only one place that kid could be, if she loves climbing trees as much as Martha says she does." The trail forked; they left the wheat field in favor of a wooded path. The sloping woods had the pungent, rich smell of black earth, the special stillness that was part of woods on an early evening. Kyle found his way unerringly to a huge old oak standing massive and proud, its thick limbs reaching toward the sky, "Joanie?" he called.

The voice that answered was so high up that Erica gasped in surprise. "Is it dinnertime? I haven't missed it, have I? Mom'll kill me." The little voice hesitated. "You Mr. McCrery? How'd you find me?"

"This was my favorite tree as a kid. I figured if you were a climber, you wouldn't settle for less than the best."

A few branches parted long enough to disclose a bright pair of blue eyes looking down at them, interested. "You sound nice."

"We are nice," Kyle assured her wryly. "Mind some company?"

"Heck, no!"

Erica blinked. One minute she was definitely on solid ground and the next Kyle's hands had hooked around her waist from behind her. "Kyle!"

"Get that first handhold, beauty."

"But I've never climbed a tree. And this one—"

"You've *never* climbed a tree?" Kyle said incredulously. "What did you do the whole time you were a kid?"

"Shopped for clothes..." Erica's hands fumbled for a hold on the branch. Kyle's hand cupped her buttocks for one last heave upward that struck her as distinctly intimate. She turned around to glare at him. The little one was giggling. "Played with dolls. Played school. Kyle—"

"Deprived childhood, it sounds like to me." He was right behind her, motioning which branches to take, shielding her body with his own so that the only place she could fall was against him.

"Exactly how high did you have in mind?" she wondered aloud.

"Heaven."

Joanie Calhoun burst into chuckles. Breathless, Erica kept climbing into the leafy haven, until she came on a level with the little girl. Joanie was a blonde with big blue yes. She was wearing jeans that could have used a wash, and she had lined up a trio of apple cores on a limb next to her. Where a single branch swayed slightly in the breeze, Erica could see the arched roofs of the barns and a long, undulating field of wheat. She'd been lower in a plane.

"Mom said you were the guy who lived in a tree as a kid," the little girl said interestedly.

"I came close; I'll have to admit that. Best place to escape from your troubles that I ever found."

Joanie concurred. The two appeared to agree on a great many things. Erica was captivated by the way Kyle handled the child, as he maneuvered up and behind her, then motioned. Erica shook her head emphatically. Kyle bent down, with feet braced against two forked limbs, and hauled her up against him, still talking to the little girl. In a moment, she was wedged in the cradle of his thighs and chest, his arms loosely supportive under her breasts. For some insane reason, she was comfortable.

"I wasn't going to like you," Joanie told him. "Mom said you made stuff out of wood. I kept thinking you'd be the kind to cut down a tree like this, just to make some dumb stuff. I think you should leave a tree a tree ..."

"I would cut off a toe before I'd touch this oak," he promised her, "but I hear you, Joanie. A tree's a special thing. Every culture that's ever existed has had a concept of the Tree of Life, and all people—no matter how different they are—have a special feeling for the trees of their land. But when I make something out of wood, I don't think of it as destroying but as creating."

"I don't get you," the little girl said flatly.

"The tree would die someday in the cycle of nature. But when something is made of its wood, that thing can last—much longer than that tree might have lived, much longer than it would take one of that tree's acorns to grow to full size. We'll skip the boring stuff we need from wood, like floors and furniture—but what about music, little one? Guitars and violins are made from

wood; those instruments last and in turn create something
that lasts—music. So that tree keeps living on, just in
a different way—you understand?"

They both understood, the man and child, with their
mutual affinity for trees. Erica leaned back against her
husband and felt his arm tighten under her breast, as
aware of her as she was of him. With his free hand, he
brushed a wisp of hair from her cheek and then let the
hand linger in the curve of her shoulder.

Her two companions refused to tire of their subject,
Kyle willingly expanding into folklore. The oak had always symbolized strength and protection. Rowan was
used as a charm against witchcraft. A witch, on the other
hand, could turn herself into an elder in a pinch; if you
cut an elder branch it was said to bleed. People used to
believe that ash cured rickets; the willow symbolized lost
love; yews represented everlasting life. "Now the hawthorn tree's a very special one," Kyle added. "If you
bring its blossoms into the house, you're risking a death
in the family. But if you sit under a hawthorn in the
middle of summer . . . you might just fall under a fairy's
spell."

"You don't believe that," said the little girl, who had
clearly believed every word. "Mom would say that was
'stitious."

"Superstitious?"

"That's what I said."

"Hmmm." Kyle shook his head, gently smiling. "I
guess I must be 'stitious then, because whenever I make
something out of oak, I get this good feeling. Like the
house it's going to will have just a little more protection
against storms, against trouble . . ."

"Really?"

Erica leaned her head back to look at him. He was
entertaining the child, but she could feel the depth of
commitment in him, a commitment based not on super-
stition, but on his love of the craft he'd taken on. She
thought of the sunburst, of the love that went into that

work, of the skill that came from the heart. And she thought of the days he'd once spent poring over dry profit and loss sheets, something he'd been very good at but that had ever really involved the core of the man she was coming to know. "Why did you leave all this?" she whispered to him.

His arm tightened around her. "Because I was eighteen and running. Because I was ashamed of all the wrong things." His eyes hovered intensely on hers, dark blue as the sky above took on evening shadows through their leafy ceiling. He hesitated, and she knew he meant to explain that . . . but they were interrupted by a bubble of laughter from below.

"Kyle McCrery, you get down from there! I'll be darned if I finally *do* get dinner on and there isn't a soul to serve it to but Leonard. I should have *known* better than to send you out after Joanie! You haven't changed a whit since you were a kid; the very first tree you see . . . Poor Erica's probably scared out of her mind, and as for you, miss . . ." She scolded the three of them like children as they followed her back to the house.

Kyle unlocked the door, and Erica stepped inside the dark house. Automatically, she slipped off her shoes and then fumbled for a lamp switch, pleasantly weary and a little bit numb from the homemade wine Martha had kept pouring for her. The small light flooded the couch where Kyle had spent a lonely night the evening before, and something chilled inside her, something she had been trying hard not to think about.

She turned. Kyle was still standing in the doorway. His hands rested loosely on his hips, and his blue eyes were intense on hers. Very quietly, he came toward her until he could place both his arms around her shoulders and press his forehead to hers.

"You want to talk about last night?" he whispered.

She shook her head. It was just there, so suddenly, a too-warm feeling as if she were about to melt inside. His sun-warmed flesh and his strength, the hair whose texture she loved, the energy that vibrated from his body, the scent of him.

"We have to, Erica."

She shook her head again.

His thumbs gently caressed the sides of her cheeks, his fingers tilting her face up to his. "You locked me out last night; you've never done that before," he whispered. "If I come upstairs, I'm going to make love to you, Erica. You know that."

She did know it, and drew back. She'd loved him, climbing that crazy tree. She'd loved hearing him laugh with Leonard, seeing him tussle with the Calhoun kids; she'd ached for him as she began to understand what raw and frightening beginnings he'd had as a child. Yet nothing could obliterate the memory of their abandoned lovemaking in the wheat field, followed only hours later by his rejecting her love as if it meant nothing to him. It wasn't that she loved him less or wanted him less, but doubt about his feelings for her made her draw back into the shadows of the room, not comfortable looking at him.

"Erica..." His face hardened, the blue eyes turned haunted.

"You said there was no love without choice. I didn't understand, Kyle...except that you made a choice the day you married me, and quite obviously you don't feel the same now—"

"And you don't either," he said swiftly. One hand slowly raked through his hair. "We're not kids anymore. That's the point. I was trying to talk about *your* choices, *your* feelings. Trying to force you to let out some of the resentment you must have felt since we moved here. Maybe I was even trying to get you angry so you would finally tell me what you were really feeling—but I didn't mean to hurt you, Erica, at least not deliberately—"

"But I've told you how I feel. A thousand times." In the wheat field, in their work, in their living together. To Erica, her feelings were so clear.

"Perhaps," Kyle said quietly. "And perhaps you told me only what you thought I wanted to hear. You're a beautiful, loving lady. Sweet, soft as silk, as elusively radiant as an opal. You'd do almost anything to avoid hurting someone's feelings."

He sucked in his breath at her silence, a stark, bleak look in his eyes. His voice hardened. "Erica, I know you. I believe I know how you feel, even if you don't have the courage to say it. I've been there, exactly in your shoes. And I don't want you living the way I lived for too many years. Trying to love, feeling resentful—"

Trying to love, she thought bleakly. Not really loving? Was it possible she had been blinded by her feelings for him so long that she'd never seen his own feelings changing?

"Erica, we've both changed," Kyle said quietly. "I feel so much at fault. At eighteen I wasn't a very honest man. Not honest with myself, not honest with you, at least not about the things that mattered to me. I'm not proud of that. But I can't be less than honest anymore. Part of that is admitting we didn't have the relationship we thought we had . . ."

"No," she choked out, and headed for the stairs. If they talked any further, she was afraid he would say out loud things she couldn't stand to hear. She wasn't ready to walk out on their marriage. She was terrified that was what he really wanted, that he was trying to tell her he had only believed he loved her.

"Erica—"

His hand closed on her wrist; she jerked free. "All I want is for things to be as they were, Kyle." When he loved her. To hell with the beach house and the luxuries, but 'at least she'd never doubted his loving her when they lived in Florida. "If we can't have that, there just isn't anything else to talk about."

He was silent then, making no move to impede her

climbing the stairs...alone. For a moment, she saw anguish carved in stark ashen color in his features, but she saw it through a blur of tears. Not wanting him to see the tears, she averted her face and escaped to the loft.

9

OUTSIDE, A DISMAL little mist of rain fell, and a blustery breeze kept snatching leaves and hurling them at the windows. "Now listen, you two," Morgan said humorously as he pushed aside his dinner plate and looked at both of them. "It's raining, so there'll be no work tonight. I think it's time we all got out of here for a little while. Let's head for a movie."

Erica glanced up from her plate at the suggestion, though it had no appeal for her. She had made every effort these last three days to work herself into the ground, and at the moment she was physically and emotionally exhausted. Neither she nor Kyle had mentioned the word *divorce,* but emotionally she felt as if she were hanging on to life by a fraying thread.

Kyle was as tired as she was, having spent every waking minute completing the roof of the new building. Abrupt and short with everyone else, he had simply been quiet with Erica. He outworked every man employed by him with a drive and single-minded determination that struck her at times as frightening; he was barely willing to stop for sleep. She worried that he wasn't sleeping . . .

And in the meantime, there was Morgan, who could visit a quadriplegic in the hospital and walk out two hours later without ever having mentioned illness. Why bother with "how are you" when a fool could see the answer was "terrible"? He made no mention of the fact that Erica and Kyle were avoiding each other like wary kittens in the same territory, and simply stepped in as if he enjoyed having the floor, a born entertainer.

And if the idea of going out to a movie had no appeal, suddenly it occurred to Erica that neither was it fair for Morgan to be continually thrust into their own pervasively glum atmosphere. She stood up from the dinner table. "We could see what's on," she suggested, handing Morgan the newspaper before she started stacking the dishes.

He found a romantic comedy that sounded campy— exactly Morgan's cup of tea. "Unfortunately, it starts in twenty minutes."

"Twenty minutes!" Erica cast an appalled look at her faded jeans. The blouse had once been a good one, a tailored, formfitting, dark crimson cotton, but there was a worn spot on the shoulder. Having showered just before dinner, she had simply snatched the first thing she found in the closet, in a hurry to have dinner ready and be prepared to work again afterward.

"You look fine, sweetheart, and you know it," Morgan admonished. "Isn't the idea for the lady to show off her figure with the clothes she puts on? More than successful, those jeans . . ."

She made a face at him. The idea of getting out had begun to seem more appealing, almost enough to put life into her features after days of numbness. And the men were hardly decked out in finery. Morgan's black turtleneck had a few years behind it, and Kyle's simple work shirt was old and soft, a honey color that rivaled his tan.

"So get some shoes on," Morgan scolded.

"I am! I am!" She scooted up to the loft for a pair of sandals, slipped them on, and hurried back down with a hairbrush in her hand. From the hall closet, she snatched a raincoat, and on her way through the kitchen, she put the broiler pan under water to soak.

"Come *on!*"

"I *am!*"

Morgan was holding the door open, letting in torrential blasts of rain, and she hurried toward him, only now realizing that Kyle was not part of the hustle. She turned with a questioning look toward him.

"No, I'm not going," he said quietly. "There's work I have to get done. Nothing that you need to be involved in, Erica."

That changed the option suddenly. Though she would have said no if Kyle had asked her one on one, Morgan's being there made it possible for the two of them to be together without friction. But going with just Morgan . . . The brightness faded a little from her eyes. Her purse slipped from her shoulder and she snatched at it. "Listen, why don't you two go, then?" she suggested. "Perhaps I can do whatever you planned on, Kyle, and there are really a thousand other things I have—"

"You go, Erica." Kyle spoke quietly, but his jaw tightened as if he were impatient with the subject.

More loyalty he didn't want? Or was she being irrationally sensitive? Yet a simple decision had somehow turned into something absurdly complex.

"Would the two of you quit fighting over my company?" Morgan complained humorously.

"Nut," she retorted, as she finally pulled up her collar and headed out the door. It was a nasty evening. The wind had a bite to it; the rain was spattering down from a cold, black sky. Morgan snatched at her hand to hurry her to his Porsche, and when she settled breathlessly in the seat and glanced back at the house, Kyle was at the window, a still, tall form without expression, his face in shadow.

For a moment, there was the sharpest pain in the region of her heart. Kyle had already turned away as Morgan started the engine, and the unfamiliar sound of such power in a car distracted her from the intense ache of loneliness she felt, both from within her and from the look of the man she was married to.

"This is luxury!"

"You'll be spoiled, I guarantee it."

She tried to be impressed with the car, to please Morgan. The seats had a soft, velvety feel, and the chrome up front glittered beneath wet street lamps as they sped along. The Porsche appeared to take corners on a dime and certainly swallowed the road, making Morgan grin like a small boy showing off. On one curve, his shoulder inevitably brushed hers, and gradually it occurred to her that she was actually alone in the car with Morgan, as if she were single, on a date.

His after shave was pervasive in the closed car, and his profile was outlined as the glow of street lights spilled in to silhouette it—a very good-looking Roman profile with just the slightest hint of extra flesh beneath his chin. The black turtleneck emphasized his blondness, and she saw a rather cruel cut to his mouth she hadn't noticed before. The gleam in his dark eyes she had always seen as softness now seemed something else. *Predatory*. It was nothing unnerving, just an awareness of how Morgan might actually be on a date, his seduction plans too carefully masked by the charm of the hours before. She shivered.

"We'll have you warm in a minute. But I can hardly believe we have to turn on a heater at the end of July."

There was a crowd in front of the small movie theater as Morgan's car pulled up. She stepped out of the car automatically, and Morgan chided her for it. "I still happen to like opening car doors for a lady. You've obviously been married too long, sexy."

She laughed, but perhaps that was the beginning of a

rather silly feeling of unease. His arm went around her shoulder to protect her from the windy rain as they waited on line, and though it was just a normal affectionate gesture, she felt disquieted again. There was a little contretemps when she pulled out her change purse to pay for her ticket, and she gave up, finally. The idea of her paying actually seemed to offend him. At the popcorn counter, they had a prolonged debate over candies—still another strangeness. Chiding herself for her oversensitivity—this was *Morgan*—she followed him into the theater as the lights were dimming.

Once the movie started, she managed to relax. The story was exactly what had been promised—a man who bedhopped was finally caught by a Little Miss Priss type. Priss was, of course, sexy as hell once she took off her glasses; the hero never knew what hit him. The story didn't have a shadow of realism to it, and the theme was antiquated, but it did have humor and warmth and lightness...abetted by Morgan, who provided a whispered running commentary next to her. "Do you believe that fool?" he hissed in her ear. "No one could be that stupid."

"The worst rakes always fall like gangbusters," she whispered back. "You just know know how happy you could be being led around on a leash, sweetheart." She had taken off her sandals and had her legs curled under her, which was the way she always watched movies. Morgan's shoulders filled the adjoining seat, and he had one leg crossed over the other; he was a husky man who took up space. He'd insisted she hold the popcorn that she hadn't wanted in her lap, and he continually reached for it. She shifted regularly. His fingers invariably brushed her thigh or stomach in the dark before they found the container of popcorn. She was sure he was unconscious of it, but she was all too aware of these intimate contacts.

When the lights went back on, Morgan groaned his displeasure over the ending. "He should have ditched her. My God, he had a terrific life before he got involved with her."

Erica shook her head with mock gravity. "He was wearing himself out, undoubtedly would have died at an early age."

"Too much sex never killed anyone," Morgan assured her wickedly. The comment ended as a whisper in her ear because he was helping her on with her coat.

"Who's talking about sex? He deserved to be murdered, a slow boil in oil. One of those jilted women was going to get smart."

It was nonsense, their dissection of the movie, but it lasted until they reached the car. The rain had stopped, but the wind was still tugging at anything not bolted down. Wisps of paper fluttered in the air, and the clouds were restless above, skimming across the night sky. Morgan had grabbed her arm and had it captured in his, his head bent a little to the wind as they walked. Now he opened the door and helped her into the Porsche, tucking in the hem of her raincoat, which had been trying to trail. "Do you mind if we just drive for a little while?" he asked her abruptly as he got in on his side.

Between a physically tiring day and the emotional weariness of too many before it, Erica was exhausted. "Of course I don't mind," she said softly. Morgan had been doing his best to entertain her and chase away the doldrums; she could hardly say no. She leaned back in the seat and closed her eyes. Her aching muscles echoed another kind of ache inside. She had a sudden picture in her mind of Kyle working alone all evening, his eyes narrowed in intense concentration, his jaw set the way it did when he had his mind totally on what he was doing.

She suddenly recalled the first movie she'd gone to with Kyle, during which he'd hidden those shoes she invariably took off. She remembered his disgusted "I guess I'll have to carry you," which he had proceeded to do to her intense embarrassment, kissing her every third step out into the darkened night until he made the mistake of stumbling, and one of her shoes popped out of his pocket . . .

Morgan stopped the car, and her eyes opened. They were nowhere, the town lights behind them. It was just a side road cradled on both sides by huge oaks and maples, their branches overhanging the pavement, wet and glistening. "Could we walk for a bit?" he asked.

It was past time to be home, but Morgan was already out of the car, waiting in front of it for Erica to join him. The night breeze was rippling the black turtleneck, and his blond hair was silvery in the moonlight. She felt a shiver of worry that seemed too ridiculous to voice, and stepped out of the car, leaving her purse on the seat. They walked along the side of the road for a while, both silent, the breeze lifting Erica's hair in sensuous swirls that tickled her throat. She dug her hands into her pockets and walked with her head down, watching the gleaming stretch of black road ahead, inhaling the sharp woodsy scents around them. She was almost unconscious of Morgan until he stopped. "Erica?"

She tilted her head up to look at him. His tone was oddly pleading, as if he were begging her to notice him. The darkness touched odd shadows on his face so that he appeared to be in pain, his cheekbones stark and his eyes in hollows. "What's wrong, Morgan?" He had been quiet for an age—Morgan who was so rarely quiet— and she had been so immersed in her own world that she had barely noticed. Inside her, guilt stirred, for the friend Morgan was to Kyle and for how little the two of them had given back to Morgan since he came here.

"Erica, just let me hold on to *someone* ... God, don't take this wrong..." The thread of anguish in his voice seemed to come out of nowhere, startling Erica far more than when he claimed her shoulders, pulling her close.

He talked of Marissa, whom he'd been seeing the previous spring. Erica had heard the name before; Morgan had even made a rare admission months before that he cared for this woman. In spite of all Morgan's playing around, Erica had understood that there might have been marriage potential there, until he'd brushed off talk of that—and the lady—when he visited in June. It was his own fault that he'd lost her, and the breach was irretrievable, but he was taking hard the loss and the loneliness.

"Erica..." His cheek nestled in her hair as he rocked her to him. The strain in his voice evoked the compassion that was so much a part of Erica's nature... yet his hold on her shoulders was so tight that her neck ached and her hair was pulling taut. She was touched that he had turned to her, and she hurt for him. Still, there was something alien, a sense of wrongness because breast and chest were pressed together, thigh and thigh... but she didn't know what to do. Not to offer comfort was unthinkable. To move away might be interpreted as rejection.

"Erica?" His head finally tilted back from hers, and she thought he was releasing her. She offered a soft smile to the dark, anguished eyes above her. You'll find someone else, she wanted to tell him, but it seemed better to offer it in silence. The caring presence of a friend was worth more than platitudes. The moonlight touched the delicate bones of her face, etched silvery streaks in her hair blowing behind her. She felt very small and very feminine in the velvet night. There was nothing but a lonely road surrounding them for miles. Her tentative smile abruptly died when she saw Morgan's head bending in slow motion toward her.

His lips touched hers once, then deepened the kiss. For seconds, she was totally still. The shock seemed to stop the flow of blood in her veins. She understood that he only needed to hold someone for a moment, that he really didn't mean anything by it. But it was not exactly that kind of a kiss. His mouth pressed harder, his hunger and urgency unmistakable, and when his hands started an exploration, so skilled, so knowing, so quickly finding the supple, smooth sides of her breasts...

She inserted her hands between them in a kind of helpless panic. Morgan pulled away immediately, step-

ping back from her. "You did take it wrong," he accused
her gently. "I'm sorry, Erica."

"I . . . of course I didn't," she assured him breathlessly. There were twelve years of friendship between
Kyle and Morgan . . . Of course she couldn't make too
much of the kiss. She could see the pulse throbbing in
his throat; his breathing was strangely harsh, guttural.
He had eyes as soft as midnight, full of apology, but
somewhere within Erica, still, stirred that sense of seeing
a predatory creature when she looked at him.

"I knew you'd understand," he said as they made their
way back to the car. Erica was shivering from the night
chill and trying not to; she kept her pace brisk, afraid he
would put his arm around her shoulder if she didn't stop
shivering. "For a long time now, I haven't come just to
see Kyle. It's been because of you, Erica. You're different from any woman I've ever been involved with.
You listen, for one thing, and yet you never seem to
judge. I'm not taking anything away from Kyle, darling.
Surely you know I see you in a completely different
way?"

He opened the door for her, and she slid in; a moment
later, he was on the seat beside her. His words were
sweet, and rationally perhaps she had understood for a
long time that Morgan wanted something special from
her in the way of friendship, apart from his friendship
with Kyle. She was a woman who posed no threat to
him, obviously. She'd never seen anything wrong with
that, anything wrong with catering to his need, for that
matter. But his embrace was something else. There was
need and there was *need,* and she was suddenly not
absolutely certain which need Morgan was talking about,
and she didn't have the least idea how to ask. Surely
that wasn't what he was talking about—Kyle's best
friend?

"It works both ways, you know." Morgan glanced at
her with a smile that brought a handsome look to his

features. "I'm ready to listen if you want a sympathetic ear, and I think you already know you can trust me."

Erica shifted uncomfortably and managed a tentative smile for him in return. He wasn't blind; she knew he was talking of her relationship with Kyle. "It's Kyle who needs that ear of yours," she temporized quietly.

"So you don't want to talk? It's all right, Erica. Just know that if there's a time you need someone—for anything—I'm here. If I'm not in town, I expect you to call me. Will you do that?"

She nodded, but his eyes had returned to the road and he didn't see the nod, so she said simply, "Yes, thank you."

She would never call him. She could not have said why, when Morgan knew her and Kyle more intimately than anyone else. It even seemed a little crazy for a moment that she didn't at least try to confide in him. Until a few minutes ago, she had believed Morgan cared for Kyle as a brother and for her as a sister, and that if any outsider could have helped with their marital problems it would be Morgan. For that matter, Morgan would surely understand her side better than anyone else would; hadn't he just confessed to loving someone who hadn't loved him in return?

But she knew she would never call, even heard the dismissive note in her voice as she thanked him. It was a closed subject, one she didn't want brought up again. Evidently, Morgan heard the tone in her voice as well, for there was an odd sound to the gears as he careened around a corner and forced the Porsche to a burst of speed on a straightaway. They were almost home.

— 10 —

A SINGLE LAMP burned in the living room when Erica opened the front door. The clock over the refrigerator told her it was eleven; the movie had been over long before ten. She glanced around seeking Kyle, but the room was empty.

For a moment, she was grateful. Her hands were trembling as she hung up her raincoat, something she wouldn't have wanted Kyle to see. It was stupid, really. Morgan had obviously never intended to make a pass, and the entire way home he had talked of nothing but friendship . . .

She wandered to the bathroom and picked up a brush. The wind had tousled her hair and turned her cheeks to coral, adding a sensual blush to her features. All she really noticed were her eyes, huge and topaz, and as skittish as those of a doe caught in a hunter's spotlight. It was that damned lonely road. It wasn't the embrace, but the unshakable feeling that Morgan had manipulated her onto that isolated country road.

Which was absolutely ridiculous.

Restlessly crossing her arms under her breast, she paced the living room for a few minutes. She wanted Kyle. Her head seemed to have jammed into reverse, because she couldn't seem to care that they had argued or that she was the one who had cut off communication; she just wanted to be with him. Her heart kept beating like a ticker tape, adrenaline pumped through her veins as if she had something to be afraid of when she knew she didn't. She paused by the window and saw a single beacon of light from a window of the old shop.

Shivering in the damp night air, Erica nearly raced across the yard. Branches sent down a spattering of rain on her hair and cheeks, and the darkness offered a number of obstacles to stumble over. Breathlessly, she opened the door to the old shop and hurriedly made her way toward that beacon of light in the back. Ghosts were on her tail, the kind of ghosts she'd had when she was seven on a very black night, and no amount of mature self-scolding seemed to chase them away. The adrenaline pump refused to slow down until she was actually standing in the doorway looking at Kyle. As if someone had slipped her a shot of brandy, she miraculously relaxed.

Kyle was bending over the wood lathe, tiny specks of wood shooting into the air around him as he worked with a familiar tense concentration. For a moment, she leaned back against the door and simply watched, loving the look of the man. She could swear Kyle's energy flowed into the material he worked with. A thick, short, ordinary plank was stuck on the lathe; under his fingers the shape gradually took on a purity and grace of line . . . The machine stopped abruptly. Kyle wiped his hands absently on his jeans, and though he couldn't possibly have heard her, he suddenly whirled around. Those turquoise eyes she loved fastened hard on hers, wary, tense, a shock of dark hair curling onto his forehead.

"Kyle?" she started hesitantly. "If I'm interrupting you . . ."

He shook his head, wiping his hands with a rag. He

was staring at her, taking in that slight breathlessness, that whiplash of sensual swirl to her hair, her shivering form without a coat. "I didn't hear the car come in."

She thought he must have. If not heard, then seen; the car lights would have shone directly in the shop's windows above his head. "I went into the house, but when you weren't there... If you're in the middle of something—"

"I was in the middle of working off a hell of a lot of mental wars, sweet." He took a breath and suddenly smiled at her, the brusque tension leaving his face. "Which I no longer seem to have, thanks to the look of you. Come on over here and check this out. In fact, you can finish it, if you want to..."

"You mean work with the lathe?" She'd never touched it before, always terrified she would destroy something he was working on.

"I know you've been curious. There's no reason you can't fool around with it any time you want to."

"Of course there is. Look, Kyle, in the eighth grade, on the aptitude tests for mechanical ability, I scored in the third percentile."

Chuckling, he nudged her in front of him, explaining the slow-turning wheels. His hands followed hers as she gradually began to understand the rhythm and motion of the machine, fascinated. "What is this perfectly beautiful thing we're creating?" she asked whimsically.

He chuckled again. "One perfectly symmetrical, uniquely crafted"—his hand smoothed her hair back to get closer as her hand slipped—"absolutely useless vase. It won't even hold water. Not the point, though, sweet. The point is just getting the chance to work with a piece of catalpa, not exactly a common wood. I could tell you why a woodworker loves it in terms of its physical properties, but much more to the point"—he nudged her hand a second time—"is that catalpa is that big old kind of tree that bursts out with clusters of flower in the spring. They call them bridal bouquets..."

"Kyle!" she said a few minutes later. She was entranced as he took the vase off the lathe and held it up to the light. It was perfect, all thin, delicate fluted edges and intricately swirling grain. Well. Almost perfect, except where her hand had slipped twice.

"This is art," she informed him impishly. "And you only get partial credit, Mr. McCrery."

His eyes were dancing at her obvious pride. "Now don't get all disappointed if it sits lopsided on a table."

"It wouldn't dare." In a flash, she darted out the back door, and returned a few moments later with a handful of dandelions. "Just stop that," she scolded Kyle, who had started laughing.

"Stop what? I always thought dandelions were classier than roses."

She arched one intimidating eyebrow. "This vase is too classy for a rose."

"I couldn't agree more. Erica?" He turned away to do a quick cleanup around the lathe, and then switched out the light. "I'm glad you came home," he said quietly.

She smiled curiously. "Of course I came home."

They walked to the door. For a moment, Erica thought he was going to swing an arm around her shoulder, something he would automatically have done before they had started tearing each other apart with their arguments. He didn't, but their eyes met that instant in the darkness, evocative somehow of the tension they both felt, a tension neither wanted to feel with the other. Yet for that short time working together, she had so easily forgotten...

"Of course you came home," he echoed lightly, "and can I take it as an 'of course' that you still want to go away for a few days, Erica?"

She'd put the proposed vacation completely out of her mind. No, she didn't want to go. She knew exactly how it would be, an idyll like their afternoon in the wheat field, destroyed hours later when he turned cold. Like the laughter when they'd climbed the tree at Martha's, like the fun they'd just had in the shop. The smallest

incidents recyled massive feelings of love for him, and
then she was stuck on the downward swing of the yo-
yo. No. Insanity would be kinder. "Convince me to go,"
were the words that came from her mouth, which was
obviously on another wavelength entirely.

"That may not be easy," he said wryly. "I'm afraid
Roman ruins and lush Corfu beaches aren't exactly an
option, Mrs. McCrery..." He talked on as they walked
the leafy path back to the house and inside. When they
were in the kitchen, he got out two wineglasses and
poured the Pinot Noir she liked, leaning back against the
counter. "Thursday's the earliest we could take off, after
the roof's done. I had the Upper Peninsula in mind, Erica.
If we rented a little two-seater Cessna, we could be in
Newberry in four hours, where we could rent a Jeep.
The kind of fancy entertainment I had in mind would
start there."

"In Newberry," she said blankly, already starting to
smile.

"In Newberry," he echoed. "At the town dump." He
waved away her giggles with a mock scowl. "You think
I'm not serious. Now most people think it's only a little
town with an airport, an unusually boring little country
town. Not so. The bears all come down from the woods
at night to raid their dump, you see, and the whole town
brings popcorn and tries for ringside seats... Now that
is an option," he said gravely, "but to tell the truth I had
in mind getting out of Newberry as fast as the speed limit
will allow."

She laughed again, taking a sip of wine. "Now wait
just a minute—"

"Close by is Tahquamenon Falls. Deep forest country,
the falls cascading down from sheer rock cliffs. You'd
like that, Erica," he coaxed gently, his voice a very soft,
low baritone. "That's Hiawatha land, where he supposedly built his birchbark canoe. Then up to Whitefish
Point. You've heard Morgan and me talk a thousand
times about ships that were lost on the Great Lakes. In

college, we planned to become millionaires by retrieving some of the treasures that were sunk and never found there. We spent part of one summer scuba-diving for treasures, practically living on the forty-foot sailboat that Morgan managed to talk his parents out of..."

He took a sip of wine, talking of ships. The Great Lakes were full of them, carrying the rich resources of the neighboring shores—iron ore and copper, lumber, furs, and later, passengers and steel. The viciousness of sudden storms was legend on the lakes...so many lost and never heard of again. "If I had a map, you could see Whitefish Point. You could see how easily a ship might desperately try to hug the shore on a stormy night, be misled, and end up smashed...but still, that's not exactly where I want to take you, Erica. No, the destination I have in mind is Vermillion."

"Vermillion." She rolled the word on her tongue. "Now I know I haven't seen that one on a map."

"Because it isn't there," Kyle agreed. "There isn't even a paved road for miles. It's just a deserted beach in the middle of nowhere...but once it was a Coast Guard station with a lighthouse and life-saving boats ready to aid a foundering ship. I swear you can imagine it when you're there, Erica..."

She could picture it now. A dozen times, without consciously listening, she'd heard the men talk on the subject, yet now the image caught—the history, the ships, the deserted beach, the ghosts of storms past in a lonely place, sunsets and silence... She looked at Kyle. "Let's pack," she suggested teasingly.

"You really want to go, Erica? I'm talking about camping out, not a luxury vacation..." He put down his glass and strode forward to lace his arms around her neck, to nudge his forehead against hers. "Let's see how it is with us there. Alone, Erica..."

In principle, she wanted to stiffen when he touched her. Passion would only cloud the unresolved issues between them, and she hadn't forgotten how he'd rejected

her love and loyalty. In the back of her rational mind,
she knew Kyle still felt attraction . . . but she doubted his
love. She'd had too many ups and downs; Kyle had too
much power to hurt her. She'd meant what she told him
a few nights before, that if he no longer felt love, she
just wanted to be left alone.

That was in principle. Reality was the mood he'd spun
with the image of the two of them alone on a deserted
beach. Another reality was the fruity taste of the wine
that lingered on his lips as they touched hers. Once.
Twice. Like an alcoholic, she wanted more of that taste,
denying its effect as an intoxicant. She could always pull
back in a moment. She was thirsty, that was all.

They were both thirsty. It seemed like a year since
she'd felt the touch of his fingers in her hair, roughly
brushing back the red-gold strands, cradling her head. A
century. His lips rubbed on hers, then his teeth grazed
her lower lips. She seemed to have caught a fever. Her
breasts were suddenly swollen and too warm, aching
against his sinewy chest. Everything ached. Her knees
felt too shaky to support her. Her throat arched as his
kiss deepened. "Kyle . . ."

"Don't tell me we don't have this," he whispered
roughly. "You make your damn choices, Erica, but don't
ever forget what we do have. I told myself I would give
you all the space you needed, but that just won't work,
sweet. I'll be damned if I'll ever spend another night like
this one. Waiting, thinking . . ."

The pressure of his mouth hurt her. It was the most
delicious hurt. Her limbs tightened in familiar anticipation and her heart slowed down to savor it. Her head
registered his strange choice of words, striking a single
swift, painful chord of fear; for that instant, she thought
he meant waiting for her because of Morgan, because he
guessed . . . but he couldn't possibly have guessed what
Morgan had done. It didn't make sense.

The feel of his springy hair beneath her fingers made
sense. She felt sad and frightened and a little angry that

he could pull her in so helplessly . . . but his holding her made sense. He was the cause of trouble . . . and its solution. Her heart found that perfectly rational; her heart had responded exactly that way from the moment she met him. They were standing in the kitchen; it didn't matter. Moonlight touched the hollows of his face through the open window; his eyes were indigo and soft and deep, hovering over hers as he pulled her closer. The more he touched, the more she felt like liquid inside, like a stream that wanted to flow in, through, all around him, drown forever the problems they could not seem to solve between them.

Before she could think, they were on their way upstairs. She was standing by the bed; his knuckles were grazing the sides of her breasts as he unbuttoned her blouse. The material fell away; before she could breathe, he had slid the straps of her bra off her shoulders, loosened the clasp. Moonlight cast a warm glow on her bare breasts . . . and then his hands covered them as he lowered her to the quilted bed.

In seconds, he had taken off his clothes, then he finished that job for her as he pulled off her jeans. She closed her eyes, feeling the weight of his body sliding down next to hers, feeling a little more of her sanity slip away. Soft kiss followed soft kiss. His lips finally deepened on hers, his tongue probing the inside of her mouth, talking to hers in that sweet, silent language of intimacy.

For an instant, he stopped and just looked at her. Turquoise eyes met topaz. And then his lips lowered again, hovering at the sensitive spot behind her ears before touching down again. Nape, neck, throat. She found her voice.

"Listen," she said weakly.

"I'm listening."

"This isn't going to solve anything."

"It certainly isn't," he agreed. He kneaded her breasts together so that he could kiss both of them at the same time, concentrating on the furrow he had created directly over her heartbeat. She was trying very hard to remember exactly why it was such a terrible idea that they make love... Because it clouded up everything else, that was it. Because he thought so little of her love and loyalty; because at core she believed he no longer loved her, because he had been trying to push her away. Because passion was a mockery without commitment...

He shifted just a little, his palm lazily teasing the length of her, over breast and down to the smooth silk of her flat stomach, to the slim roundness of her hip, to the long expanse of her thigh. She could feel the helplessness invade her like sweet heat in her bloodstream.

"Do you want to talk about it?" he murmured.

"Pardon?"

"Do you want me to stop, Erica?" he asked gravely.

She heard that somber note in his voice. Her eyes flickered open. His were just above her, full of the very devil. He knew exactly what he was doing to her.

"Let's discuss it...in a little while," she suggested, just as gravely. "Like nine o'clock tomorrow morning."

He smiled, his touch softening, his hand gently combing her hair. "Erica. If you really..." he said seriously.

He deserved a little of his own medicine. Her fingers inched up to his chest, to his broad neck, to the silky thickness of his hair. Gradually, her hands found their way back down again, taking in the long slope of his shoulders, the way his supple flesh lent itself to kneading in her hands. She loved his skin. She loved the way his body responded to her simplest touch. She loved the way he was made, his thighs as taut as iron, his hips so narrow, the spirals of hair covering his chest. She knew exactly what to do to send this man over the edge, and she loved doing it.

Something changed along the way. Kyle had never been happy unless he was active. His hand found its way to the soft skin of her inner thighs, fingers seeking secrets, finding them. His mouth covered hers and didn't let go. She found herself holding on, off-balance, her breathing hard and erratic; she had the sensation of being halfway through a roller coaster ride where the next slope was dizzyingly in sight. It was forever before he ended that kiss, something started in exquisite tenderness blending with a fierce erotic pressure that demanded her response. Demanded... yet coaxed.

Gradually, his mouth left hers again, and his palm slid back up the length of her, a fingertip smoothing her bruised lips, which his own had just left. "I really don't think you want to do this," he murmured huskily. "You wouldn't have been sleeping alone if you wanted to do this..."

She reached up to silence him with her lips on his. Finally releasing his mouth, she said, "You said something disgustingly similar the first night I woke up next to you."

"You were a virgin." He nibbled at her neck. "God knows how you had maintained that status." He nibbled at the other side of her neck. "Actually, it scared the hell out of me."

"You never told me that."

"What if I had hurt you? The last thing I wanted to do was hurt you, sweet. I just wanted to make love to you. Twenty-four hours a day."

"You did," she commented idly, loving his smile. But he didn't really mean that smile. They were both trying to prolong a pleasure that could have erupted too easily and been lost. Part of the sweetness of marriage was knowing each other that way, and that well. There was a time for a fifteen-minute love session, and a time for lovemaking that took hours. "Kyle..."

She didn't want to wait for hours. She wanted him at that moment more than life. He shifted over her, crushing her swollen breasts to his chest. Her hands were feverish up and down his back, the longing an insistent rhythm, a bittersweet anguish of need. His skin was so warm, both familiar and brand-new, his arousal like fire between them.

For one last instant, he drew back to look at her. The teasing in his eyes had been replaced by an intensity that burned as he surveyed the restless color in her cheeks, the luminous gold in her eyes, the moonlight burnishing a gold on the cream of her skin. For a moment, they were both still, and Erica felt a shiver that trembled all through her. Suddenly she was unsure. They both knew what was to happen; it wasn't that. It was the sudden fierce possessiveness in his eyes, a need so stark it seemed almost desperate... Instinctively, she reached up to touch his cheek in the darkness. "Kyle, you didn't force me here. I wanted to be here, with you... like this."

"God, I need you. I don't know how to tell you, Erica..."

There was no more play, no more languid, sensual climb. The urge was to join, a mutually primitive drive as basic as breath... as love. Their mating was how she had always understood their marriage at core. He was the stronger, with powers distinctly male, his control dominant and deliberate in love as it was in life... but it was when he lost his control that Erica burst inside.

She complemented him perfectly. Her powers were distinctly feminine. She could cloak his strength inside her softness, take his fierce drive within her. She gave him everything; it was her nature. She drew from him his strength, his power, his control, his protection. Her trust was total, and had been from the beginning; she felt cherished in his keeping, which was the reason he was able to take her so high, the reason she felt freed in loving...

He brought tears to her eyes, a cry from her lips... and then he simply held her, their bodies still joined, their hearts beating in the same triumphant rhythm, gradually slowing at the same pace.

The night finally settled silence on both of them. Erica's cheek rested on his shoulder, her limbs were entwined with his, and the cool sheet cocooned them in a private world. Kyle slept. She thought again, her eyes wide open in the darkness, that their mating was their marriage. Their lovemaking had always worked; at the worst of times, other emotions had intruded, but he had never failed to demand—and receive—the most from her, knowing her secrets. A woman's body was created with secrets, none of which she could keep and be a woman. That she understood, and she understood, too, that her loving him was right, so enmeshed in her nature that it was as instinctive as desire, as wanting and needing and breathing.

It would not just...smash. If there was really so much terribly wrong with their marriage, their loving should not have worked. It made no sense. Kyle's touch was loving, had never failed to be loving through their whole crisis together. She held on to that long into the night.

— 11 —

IT WAS JUST past three. Erica could not remember a Wednesday so quiet. Kyle had sent the men home, this time for good. Whatever still had to be finished on the new building they could do themselves. An hour before there had been shouts of congratulations and satisfaction, and then sounds of engines starting as the men left.

Now there was no one but herself, not even a sign of Morgan or Kyle. Erica had grown so accustomed to the sounds made by hammers and saws and power tools that the quiet seemed strange. She'd stood in the doorway for an age watching the men take off in their trucks. They were mostly college students. It wasn't a town that had an abundance of summer employment for school kids, beyond those whose parents needed them on their own farms. They had been a good group. They had complained loudly that Kyle was a slave driver, and he had complained loudly that they didn't know a nail from a screwdriver, which they had vigorously and in detail protested when Erica was not supposed to be within hearing range.

She'd offered to make lunch for the entire group more

than once, but they'd preferred to cart their girl friends
to the site, eating sandwiches sprawled on the grass,
preferably as nearly naked as possible. They worked the
same way, though she guessed the heat wave was not so
much a factor as their vanity. They wanted to get the
darkest tan possible to impress the girls. On the job,
though, they had caved under to Kyle, put their all into
the work, and what good-natured complaints had been
shouted did not take away from the essential respect they
had shown him.

He'd earned that. She'd never seen him fail to earn
the respect of the people he worked with, but the kids
were still something special. They were amateurs, and
they made mistakes, but Kyle had developed a sense of
pride in them as they learned. It was *their* building; she
knew they felt that way as she walked toward it now.
The anticipation and frenetic pace of weeks had finally
peaked.

Lord, she was proud of him.

The lemon sun shimmered on the new windowpanes,
on the rough grayish siding that blended right into the
wooded area beyond. Kyle had known exactly what he
wanted and had done it, and the new building was a fine,
tasteful structure that still had the scent of newness to it,
the stuff of which dreams are made. She opened the door,
imagining a customer doing it, imagining a hundred cus-
tomers doing it. Teak and mahogany, catalpa and pine,
oak, of course, even wicker from willows... First, the
customer would see finished products, from sculptures
to cabinets, each fashioned from the wood that most
suited its form and function.

A compact, well-lit office was just beyond. Erica
walked through, imagining the finished floor where there
were only bare boards now, seeing in her mind's eye
displays on the walls where there was nothing yet, imagining samples of wood, the unique tools of the trade...
Her sandals clicked on the floor as she walked through.

Kyle was standing at the very back of the building,

staring out the window with his hands on his hips and his head high. He turned when he heard her footstep. There was no smile on his face, but a look of satisfaction was in his eyes. The moment's triumph and his dreams were emblazoned there. She caught her breath when he so naturally reached out his hand for her.

She covered the last few steps with a radiant smile and took his hand.

"You see my lumberyard, don't you? That'll be part of it, in the long run." He pointed out the window. There was, of course, nothing there. A cleared space where a good-sized truck could back in to unload supplies. The drive was gravel, not asphalt yet. A rather scruffy stand of poplars was beyond that, and then a nice little stand of oak, hickory, and maple.

"I see it."

"It's so damned big it cuts out my view of the woods," he complained.

She reached up to hug him, long and hard, and then moved away quickly, not wanting anything that was between them to spoil his moment of dreams.

Both men were in the backyard when she came out with a tray of lemonade at four-thirty. They were both lying back in lounge chairs, half in shade, half in sun, both stripped down to cutoff jeans and bare feet. Both claimed they were moving nowhere for the rest of the day, but they energetically hooted down her lemonade in favor of something alcoholic.

She returned a few minutes later with a second tray, bearing glasses and a full pitcher of a celebratory screwdrivers, more vodka than orange juice, and again faced the two stretched-out figures who refused even to open their eyes. "Will this suit?" She pressed an ice-cold glass directly to Kyle's stomach. He groaned just as Morgan did with similar treatment. "Do you think you can rouse enough energy to drink it? I mean, you'll actually have to raise your heads," she said with mock sympathy.

"Sit down and relax, General," Morgan ordered.

"Actually . . ." Her eye rested on a monarch butterfly as it flitted gracefully through the yard. Then on Kyle, who had been so relaxed with her today that she felt the delicious urge to pounce on him, liberated hormones like tantrums in her bloodstream. Then she looked at Morgan, whose eyes had slitted open just enough to take in the snug white shorts she wore, and the bright yellow top that showed every curve. Quickly, her eyes skimmed away from Morgan to rosebushes she had been trying to grow. She had planted some delicate white flowers, whose name eluded her for the moment, as well. The scent of the white flowers came out only at night, an overpowering perfume next to the window. Then her glance flickered back to Kyle again, to the way his jeans fit over his thighs, to his smooth forehead with its boyish shock of black hair, to his fine Irish nose and the broad bones in his cheeks, to his dark eyebrows so shaggy that they shaded his eyes in sunlight. As if he knew she was watching him, Kyle suddenly opened his eyes, a startling turquoise next to his tanned skin. To her dying day, those eyes would evoke bedrooms. She glanced deliberately back to the garden. "Actually, I think I'll do a turn at those weeds in the garden . . ."

Morgan groaned. "Where did you *get* her?" he complained to Kyle.

"Where did I get her?" Kyle echoed lazily, and leaned back with his arms behind his head, eyes closed. "I picked her up at a third and seventeen in the fourth quarter of a Cotton Bowl game. Literally. Surrounding her was the cream of the freshman class, the female portion, all dressed to the teeth and demurely chugging their sterling flasks. Not Erica. She was standing on the bench shouting her head off. Do you have any rope?"

Morgan denied it. "There might be some in the shop."

"Too far to move, unfortunately. We could have tied her to the chair. Erica, just *see* if you can manage to sit still for a full fifteen minutes. You might even decide it feels good for a change. As I was saying..."

She threw a look of mock disgust at both of them. After a moment, she poured herself a screwdriver and flopped obediently into a lounge chair between them. It was so poignantly reminiscent of other times, when there were no troubled waters, no ships floundering. She would have stood on her head to ensure that nothing marred this day for Kyle, feeling the simplest pleasure at just seeing him being lazy and...easy. Leaning back, she closed her eyes.

"Some drunk was trying to get past her, and Erica didn't see him. She was too busy shouting down to the coach, telling him how to run his team—"

"Kyle," she scolded absently. Morgan was already chuckling. God knew why. He had heard the story a thousand times before.

"I was just passing, but I'd stopped at the rail to watch that critical play before I went back to my seat—which, you may remember, Shane, I worked night and day to pay for, and it was still nowhere *near* the fifty-yard line where Erica and her upper-crust friends were sitting. Anyway, the next thing I know she's flying off the seat—"

"Gross exaggeration," Erica murmured.

"There's no point in interrupting," Morgan scolded wryly.

"*NO ONE ELSE*," Kyle said loudly, "seemed to know what to do with her. I mean, what *do* you do with a girl who seems to be upside down in the middle of the stadium where the rest of the crowd—even the drunks—are right-side up and screaming...One of the classic pass interceptions in football history, and I missed it. In fact, I missed the entire rest of the game. *Someone* had to sponge her off. Half the sterling flasks in the crowd had contributed a dribble or two on her way down. She had a bump on her forehead the size of a goose egg—"

"Have you noticed how the size of that bump grows from year to year?" Morgan muttered in an aside to Erica.

". . . smelled like a liquor factory, had a run in her stockings, and was so hoarse from all her solo cheerleading that she could barely croak for the next two hours. I had to carry her fireman-style to the first-aid station . . ."

"Why did you have to get him started?" Erica demanded plaintively to Morgan.

She should not have sat down. There had been too many weeks of almost nonstop work; now her limbs felt glued to the lounge. She felt cradled in, cocooned both by simple tiredness and by the memories Kyle was invoking. She could so easily close her eyes and see the Kyle McCrery of nine years ago, wickedly attractive, looking far too old for her at first glance, and very definitely a total stranger. He had not carried her firemanstyle, but he might as well have, ignoring her hoarse objections as he hustled her through the crowds, burrowed her into a little room she would never have guessed existed, and brushed the first-aid attendant's administrations aside in favor of his own. He had made her lie down on the cot and told to close her eyes. Then he gently placed a damp cloth on the bump on her forehead, and suddenly he was unbuttoning her beautiful aquamarine suit, and her eyes had opened as wide as saucers.

"The front of your suit was all damp. I was just trying to . . ." She hadn't believed him then, and she didn't now, but he had buttoned the suit up again . . . for a time. They were both students at the University of South Florida in Tampa, so it was not all that surprising they had found their way to the Cotton Bowl at the same time. What was surprising was how fast it all happened. At the time, in that little first-aid station, she was mortified at being such a mess and exasperated at missing the game . . . and completely captivated by those Irish blue eyes, so possessive on hers. She knew in every virginal bone exactly what he had in mind . . .

"She's asleep," Morgan said quietly.

"She's exhausted."

"She's lost weight; there are hollows under her eyes, and she's been trying to work until she drops, McCrery. Naturally, she's exhausted."

But she didn't hear Morgan's low digs, couldn't hear the subtle note in his voice that had dug under Kyle's skin over and over, didn't see the look on Kyle's face, the sudden tension. She was replaying that moment in the past, dreaming it over and over again. The suit had been a favorite but too warm for the day; she had worn no blouse, only a silky little camisole beneath it that hugged every womanly curve. Someone *had* spilled whiskey on the lapel; the scent *was* strong; it was not inconceivable that Kyle had unbuttoned her jacket only to sponge it off. Nor would a little silk camisole have shocked a fast-moving man like Kyle McCrery; she owned bikinis that showed a great deal more of her. But the feeling was there, that instant. The feeling that her innocence was laid bare to him, and Kyle told her with his eyes that he was claiming that innocence. She recalled that delicious sense of fear and anticipation in her mind, remembering the silent little speech she had delivered to herself, that there was no excuse for naiveté in this life, that rockets didn't really go off...

A shotgun exploded, and then another and another. Erica's eyes flew open. The other two lounge chairs creaked as Kyle and Morgan launched themselves out of them and took off at a dead run for the new building. There was another volley of gunshots and then a crazy, raucous hooting of horns—car horns, truck horns, hunters' duck horns, whistles, cat calls—so absurdly grating on the ears that Erica covered hers as she started running, too. She had in mind bombs, robbers, terrorists...

Suddenly, she saw Martha Calhoun coming toward her. Erica could hear Martha's laughter even above all

the other noises. "Come *on!*" she exhorted with a wild
motioning of her hands.

"What on *earth* is going on?" There were people
everywhere suddenly: the boys Kyle had hired and their
girl friends, their parents, Martha's family, vaguely remembered faces like Mr. Hendriks from the grocery and
the mailman, a Mrs. Polanataz who had brought them a
cake the day they had moved here, neighbors and cus-
tomers... Fireworks were being set off in the yard, and
the new building was still surrounded by men with guns.
None of the people were empty-handed; they were carting
everything from packaged potato chips to homemade potato salad. One pickup truck had been backed up to the
front door of the new building and clearly held a keg of
beer, the bed of the truck dripping with ice blocks to
keep it cold. Kyle and Morgan were already there, laughing, their heads thrown back—and a roar of approval
went up when they enthusiastically downed the first paper
cupful of beer. Kyle caught sight of her and motioned
her to his side, but it just wasn't that easy to get through
the people in an instant.

Martha grabbed Erica's arm and hugged her with ex-
citement, shouting at the top of her lungs for her son to
keep away from the beer. "It's a belling," she announced.
"An old German custom—though, as you know, I haven't
a drop of German blood, but then the Irish were never
ones to be prejudiced where a party was concerned. The
idea is a surprise welcome to the newcomers in a neighborhood, usually honeymooners. Oh, well, I had to twist
the rules a bit in other ways, too. A belling's supposed
to take place after dark, but Leonard has to be back for
the milking by seven. And it's hardly your first day in
the neighborhood, but we thought that new building
needed a christening and maybe we just all needed an
excuse to support you two. Anyway, if you can picture
how it's *supposed* to be—the husband-to-be with his
virgin bride; he's finally got the lights out and her clothes
off, and all of a sudden there's an explosion of noise,

and they're expected to come down pronto, entertain perhaps fifty people who all bring food and drinks and are prepared to keep the couple from . . . uh . . ."

Erica burst out laughing as Martha finally ran out of breath.

"The idea died out around thirty years ago," Martha admitted. "God knows why. Everybody jumped to take part when I called. It's been on my mind for an age. You see, the last one I heard of was organized by Joel McCrery, and he did it up right, on the night my parents were married. I wasn't, respectfully, born then—but I've heard about it for years. I've just been itching for an excuse—"

"You sweetheart!" Erica said warmly.

"You probably won't say that later. Everyone's supposed to bring their own refreshments, but a blind bat could see they've brought more bottles than food. I can just picture the mess a few hours from now!"

Erica could see it with her own eyes, those few hours later. The noise and confusion and hilarity had just died a few minutes ago, and Kyle and Morgan were sprawled next to her with their backs propped up against packing crates. The litter in front of them included an incredible variety of debris—half-eaten cakes, half-empty bottles, enough crackers and cheese to last a year, an empty, dripping keg . . . and in one corner, an eighteen-year-old boy sleeping peacefully with his head cradled in his hands, snoring.

"I'm going to have to take him home," Kyle said ruefully, but he made no immediate movement to get up.

"You know where he lives?" Morgan questioned.

"On the other side of town."

"Naturally."

There was a definite hierarchy of intoxication in the room. The worst was obviously the boy, then Morgan and Erica, and last, Kyle. Morgan, who by nature livened up a party, was one of few this time who had not been in a celebratory mood. Though he'd drunk every toast to Kyle and the new venture, he'd offered none, and his head was bent down in moodiness now...or perhaps headache.

Erica had joined the hilarity with gusto, quickly separating from Martha to take over as hostess. She'd glowed, showing people through both new building and old. The support and enthusiasm and warmth the people showed to Kyle warmed her inside, filling her with pride in her man for the respect he'd earned, and the way people just seemed naturally to like him made her want to gravitate toward him.

She was not fond of beer, but it was hardly the time to be picky when her husband was being toasted. So she had drunk more than she wanted to, and now there was a slight cast of double vision everywhere she looked...but it was not the beer that had altered her mood three-quarters of the way through the party. Perhaps it was the way Morgan kept looking at her oddly every time she turned around; perhaps it was the moment Kyle's arms were around her and they were cheered as a couple... Suddenly, as on the downgrade of a roller-coaster ride, her heart had stopped for a single beat, and then she had heard the sound of her own laughter, high and joyous.

The whole day had been upbeat, as if nothing were wrong...but of course, that was an illusion. She was bubbling on about Kyle's plans as if she were a part of them; the whole boisterous welcome to the neighborhood included her...and yet it didn't. For the last few days, Kyle had been so much the energetic, spirited, dynamic man she married that she had almost forgotten—or tried to forget—that she wasn't sure how long she was going to be in this cozy small town in Wisconsin. How long did he want her there?

Choices; we can't go on the way we have been; there's no love without active choice...Her laughter, so right and easy moments before, was suddenly a sham, and a hollow ache had wrenched inside as she saw herself as hostess to a celebration she had no right to.

Kyle stood up abruptly and viewed the sleeping boy with hands on hips, wry smile on his face. "God knows I should have seen it coming. Johnny never was away from the keg, but I don't know what I'm going to tell his parents." He shook his head in rueful exasperation, glancing at Erica.

She lurched up to a standing position, absently touching her fingertips to her temples at the unexpected dizziness, swearing off beer in the afternoon for the rest of her life. Silently. "I'll help you get him to the truck, and then I'll go after this mess."

"Hell—just relax, Erica; it isn't going anywhere," Morgan insisted. "I'll help with the boy," he said curtly to Kyle.

The two men managed to half carry the boy to Kyle's truck while Erica started trying to make sense of the chaos. The late afternoon sun faded in dusty shadows on the debris, not the best of mood-breakers. She started carting trash bags out to the back, each cumbersome but none heavy. She was in a hurry suddenly. She wanted the room cleared, back the way it was earlier that afternoon, when the scent of brand-newness had touched her: newness had hope in it.

So had she. Kyle had been so loving the night before . . . She thought of the intricately carved vase, of the half-finished sunburst; she thought of that crazy moment when he had vaulted her up into the tree at Martha's.

But nothing was quite that simple. He cared; she had never believed he hated her. They were not *enemies*. Yet she knew in her heart that his feelings had changed for her since they moved here; he had excluded her from every decision that counted. He didn't want to speak of his real feelings . . . It was a little too easy to make a lot out of shared passion on a single night. If the man didn't love her, she couldn't stay.

An exasperating tear spilled onto her cheek as she battled with the last of the bags. Her head ached from the beer, and the late afternoon sun seemed curiously

harsh, eye-blinkingly bright, showing up the emptiness
of the rooms that had been filled with dreams before.

"Oh, Erica..."

Morgan was next to her in long, swift strides. She
had completely forgotten him, assuming he had gone
with Kyle to help with the boy. The deep, husky sympathy in his voice was the last straw; not to mention
being caught in the midst of tears, weariness, the wretched
beer hangover. He had his arms around her in seconds,
stroking her hair, listening to her cry. "I *hate* to see you
so unhappy. And I hate to see you doing things like this!"
He made a motion that encompassed her efforts to pick
up after the party, which seemed relevant to absolutely
nothing.

"It was the stupid beer," she tried to say, desperately
trying to stop crying.

"It wasn't the beer. You deserve more than this, Erica.
I know the life you were meant for, and it wasn't this.
I've been waiting and waiting for you to see it..."

She barely heard him as she snatched the handkerchief
he offered, mopping at her face and taking great gulping
breaths. It worked. The tears stopped, though her control
was still shaky. She felt even shakier as she suddenly
realized that Morgan's arm was still possessively around
her, and heard something disquieting in the tone of his
voice. It occurred to her that Morgan was very, very
drunk.

"I *need* you, Erica. Surely you've known that for an
age? And no more working yourself ragged, no more
living on hamburger, no more being stuck in this little
burg..."

Suddenly, he sounded too much like Morgan and not
enough like a drunk. Confused, she saw his eyes above
hers, fever-bright, aimed like darts, and she felt every
nerve ending in her body recoil...

It was just too much. She couldn't cope with the
harshness of sunlight, much less instantly bounce back

from the despair she felt as a result of the difficulties between herself and Kyle. The last thing on her mind was old lessons on how to treat a man as villain. And Morgan was no villain; he'd offered comfort so many times as a friend; he'd given Kyle his time and back-breaking work... She simply didn't know how to begin a wrestling match with him now.

"Morgan—"

She felt a bleak helplessness inside when his lips pressed on hers, when he roughly tried to mold her stiff form closer. Almost detached, she realized what he was doing, noted that his fingers were frenetic in an effort to arouse her sexually. Arrogant hands, so full of confidence... In that single instant, she saw a thousand flashbacks: affection she had innocently invited, sexual innuendos she had unwittingly parried, touching allowed that could be interpreted as her wanting and needing Morgan. She *had* wanted him—for Kyle. Not for herself. Never in that way.

"Please—"

His mouth tasted like the beer he had had too much of. It was distasteful to her, smothering. Her own guilt almost numbed her... yet not enough. The shorts and top she wore were insufficient covering against the onslaught of his hands, determined on intimacy, claiming her breasts, twisting in her hair, sweeping over her stomach to her hips. Fear warred with a feeling of nausea, of panic. He was far stronger than she was, and his roughness caused her to shake. Her frantic breathing seemed to give him all the wrong messages.

"Morgan!"

"You're trembling, Erica," he hissed. "You didn't think it would be that way only with Kyle, did you? I knew... I knew..."

"*Stop* it! Let *go!*" She pushed desperately with her hands, wrenching away from him.

Morgan took a step back, breathing heavily, his eyes

black with arousal, running his fingers through his thick
mat of blond hair. His shoulders arched back as he stared
at her, seeing her arms locked protectively across her
chest, her wild mane of hair, her blouse hanging open
where a button had popped. Her eyes stared at him disbelievingly, waiting for the apology that didn't come.

He leaned back against the wall, lazily shifting his
feet forward. "I think we can safely take it that you're
not in the mood," he murmured wryly. His smile suddenly slid across his face like a shutter, masking that
predatory look in his eyes, inviting her to be calm and
make light of it.

She didn't smile. "Don't...touch me again. Ever,
Morgan," she said in a low, menacing tone.

He didn't like that, and his dark eyes suddenly flickered with steel. He shook his head, still smiling. "Kyle
and I go back a long time, Erica," he said roughly. "But
if you're not with him, I have no obligation to hide my
own feelings. The marriage isn't working anymore—or
do you want to try to tell me that everything's fine between the two of you?" His tone was so heavily sarcastic
that she flinched. "It's obvious that it's over."

She could feel the color drain from her face. Was it
obvious that her marriage was over? She had thought it
a well-guarded secret and still couldn't believe it herself.

"So you thought that gave you certain rights?" she
demanded bitterly. "I don't love you, Morgan; I could
never love you that way." He took a step forward, and
she stiffened. "Just leave me alone. I thought you were
Kyle's friend—"

"Friend! As if Kyle needed one! He's always gotten
every damned thing he went after." Morgan took a rasping breath. "Don't be a fool, Erica. You're shook up,
maybe, but you know I really care for you. You know
what I can give you—"

"Nothing," she said tightly. "Ever." She saw the cold
black glint in his eyes again and felt a chill run through

her body. "I want you to go home. Leave us alone." She saw his eyes riveted below her neck and snatched shakily at the torn yellow fabric of her blouse. "Morgan, please. I don't want to tell Kyle. I don't want him to know. Please, just go away—"

"Tell Kyle," he suggested, very softly. "You think he'll believe you, Erica? You're so absolutely sure he wouldn't believe something entirely different happened? That we'd both had our share to drink at the party..."

With a sick sense of horror, Erica started backing away from him, edging toward the door of the shop. What *would* Kyle believe? Kyle had always trusted Morgan; it was only his wife he'd pushed out of his world lately, as if he could no longer trust her. Behind her, her fingers reached for the doorknob and curled around it, something solid in a very shaky world. "You wouldn't do that. You wouldn't suggest anything like that to Kyle—"

"Are you asking me not to?"

For a price, she thought bitterly. "I'm asking you to leave us both alone."

"And I will, Erica. I intended to leave in the morning, regardless. You know that. There isn't any problem, unless you create one."

He smiled. She felt nauseated. She spun around and wrenched open the door, leaving it ajar as she stumbled out into the yard toward the house. She was halfway there when she heard the engine of Kyle's truck.

It was like a nightmare. She wanted so desperately to run to him, to throw her arms around him and be sheltered and soothed... Yet she stood stock-still for that instant, too terrified that Morgan would take his revenge, and that Kyle wouldn't believe her.

In the next instant, she lost that choice. Kyle was a statue, freezing halfway out of the truck when he spotted her. He didn't so much as move, taking in the torn blouse, her tousled hair and tear-streaked face... She caught the deadly chill in his eyes before he averted his face and turned toward the open door of the new building where Morgan stood.

The truck door slammed. In tears, she ran for the house.

12

ERICA SAT AT the small dressing table in the loft where she usually put on her makeup. For an hour, she had been waiting to hear Kyle enter the house. She'd all but thrown off the clothes she'd been wearing, listening. She'd showered, listening. She put on a simple white shift and sat down, still listening.

It seemed unbearably warm and she threw her head forward, lacing her fingers behind her neck to lift off the heavy weight of hair. She ought to get it cut. When she'd first met Kyle it had been cap-curl short; he had coaxed her into letting it grow until haircuts had become trims, and finally only Kyle took the scissors to even it. Her mane, he called it on occasion. Hair! she shrieked silently. The last thing on her mind was hair...

She kept watiting, ready to spring up the moment she heard his footstep downstairs. She had a dozen speeches prepared...

Kyle, I don't care what it looked like. Please listen...

Kyle, your best friend attacked me...

Kyle, I wrecked that yellow blouse on a nail; the thing just ripped. Wasn't that stupid?

Kyle, I love you.

141

Where *was* he? What was he thinking? Another half-hour passed, and still he didn't come. Restlessly, Erica got up and walked to the window. Dusk had already fallen. She couldn't see Morgan's trailer, but the truck was no longer parked in its customary spot, nor was Morgan's car. She stood and stared until it was too dark to see, and then moved aimlessly to the bed. She didn't often have headaches, but at the moment her temples were pounding so badly it hurt to move. She lay down and stared at the ceiling. Her whole body felt like a massive electrical system on overload. Anxiety overload. Only gradually did that emotion shift to anger.

She'd be damned if she was going to lose Kyle because of Morgan. Problems between herself and Kyle . . . perhaps. But not Morgan. *That* man . . . She'd scrubbed and scrubbed in the shower, trying to get rid of the sensation of being forced, the humiliating horror of being helpless. Over and over, she'd relived her own guilt in the ugly morass. Could her own actions have led him to believe she was interested? The hugs she'd thought meant to be only affectionate . . . She played all of it over and over in her brain. Perhaps he had misinterpreted her actions, but she had intended only friendship. It mattered.

But nothing mattered now except her own relationship with Kyle. She closed her eyes. Anger was soothing the terrible anxiety. Anger had always been missing before; she hated the emotion and gave it a wide berth. She shook at the first shouted word, would a thousand times prefer to turn the other cheek. Assertiveness was a nice buzzword, easier said than done.

For more than six months, she'd tiptoed around Kyle, believing he needed her understanding, forcing no issues because she was afraid of the answers. Those tactics hadn't worked, and she wanted her mate back. She'd remained passive, being gentle and careful and tentative. Softness was just a little too much of a luxury now. She was no child. She knew what she wanted.

She remembered the look on Kyle's face in the truck

as he caught sight of her standing in the yard, her blouse
ripped . . . Were they together at the moment? Was Morgan telling him . . . ?

She and Kyle had gained ground in a thousand ways,
she thought fleetingly. When they'd made love; the dozen
little incidents when they'd found themselves happy together; she'd learned of his background from Martha,
and several times she'd thought he was trying to open
up, tell her his feelings . . . She wasn't going to lose him
because of Morgan, and she didn't care what Morgan
told him.

Of course she did. Because if Kyle thought she had
been unfaithful . . .

Heartsick, she thought about fighting and felt like
crying. Her eyes stayed closed.

Bright sunlight streamed in onto the bed. Erica's eyes
fluttered open, and she came to immediate wakefulness
when she found herself staring at Kyle's sleeping face,
as she felt the weight of his arm around her. She didn't
breathe for a moment. Deep shadows were etched beneath his eyes; his clothes were strewn all over the floor.
The sheet barely covered his hips as if he'd hardly cared
the night before if he was covered or not. So he had
come to bed in exhaustion. But he had come . . .

Silently, she edged out from under his arm and got
out of bed. Padding to the bathroom, she ran a comb
through her hair and brushed her teeth, then drew on
panties and a pair of crisp white jeans. Her heart was
doing triple time as she walked back to the bed and sat
down gingerly next to Kyle's hip. She took a breath
before running her fingertips up his chest. He didn't stir.
But his blue eyes opened promptly enough when her bare
breasts brushed his chest and her lips found the hollow
between his bristly chin and his neck.

"Good morning," she murmured. "It's seven o'clock,
Kyle. Thursday. We have a date with a Cessna at ten,
and neither of us has packed item one."

He said nothing, just stared at her with sleep-laden
eyes. There was no smile to match her own, just an effort
to waken, to reach out from the disorientation of sleep.
She pressed a kiss in the hollow of his throat again and
then stood up, stretching with all the lazy sensuality of
an accomplished stripper. Well... amateur stripper.

The instant flare of turquoise in his eyes said she
wasn't doing too badly. Before he really woke, before
he remembered... anything, she went on talking as she
opened and closed drawers. "I thought I'd just pack a
few clothes in duffel bags. We won't need much. I have
to take the cat to Martha's. *Don't* say anything; I'm not
leaving Nuisance out if it rains. I know you've got a tent
somewhere; I aired out the sleeping bags yesterday morning. I never thought to go to the bank. Did you get
money?"

She turned, still smiling. He was no longer impressed
with her bare breasts gleaming in golden sunlight, with
her hair like fire brushing against her shoulders, with
the snug jeans she had chosen for exactly what they did for
her thighs and bottom. Betrayal was in his eyes, a chill
so cold, an accusation, a silence... She turned back to
the drawers, neatly folding the few things she needed on
top of the dresser. Her heart had plummeted to the lower
depths...

"Are we going to be able to get fishing equipment
into the plane? I thought I'd put together a box of staples.
Drinks and peanut butter... the kind of stuff we'd need
to eat outside. Paper plates. Where we're going doesn't
exactly sound like restaurant country. Did you hear the
weather report yesterday? It's supposed to be hot—"

"Erica..."

She lifted her chin stubbornly, as she turned one more
time from putting the last of her clothes in the small bag.
She lifted it. "Would you believe this is all I need? I
figured a change of jeans and a couple of tops." Her
voice was faltering in spite of herself. "I'll wear tennis

shoes and take along a pair of sandals. I'll put your stuff
together as soon as I've made us both some breakfast..."

"What the hell are you playing at?" He had lurched
up to a sitting position in bed, his bare chest soaking in
the morning sun, his black hair tousled and boyish. But
there was nothing boyish about his face, his eyes. His
look was grim, and his shoulders were tense, and his
blue eyes pierced hers, trying to make sense of her magpie chatter. "You seem to be under the impression we're
going somewhere together this morning," he interrupted
harshly.

Her stomach promptly made three somersaults. She
turned away quickly, absently running a hand through
her hair. "I think that's really all I have to remember, Kyle. There shouldn't be any trouble getting it
all together in a couple of hours. I'll make bacon and
eggs—"

"Erica—"

She beamed a radiant smile at him from the doorway.
"Obviously, though, I'll have to get on the stick if we're
going to be ready on time—"

"You are not going anywhere."

"We are, dammit!"

Her furious tone seemed to come out of nowhere,
startling Kyle. That cold-blooded stare of his seemed to
die as he became aware of exactly what her cheerfulness
cost her. No matter what he believed she had done, she
knew he was reacting to her, to Erica, to years of shielding his lady from trouble she couldn't handle. Mixed
emotions seemed to run through his head, and then he
sighed, running a hand through his hair as he looked at
her. "All right, we are," he agreed grimly. "God knows
we're not going to solve anything at this particular moment. Here. Now." Almost reluctantly, a faint hint of a
smile touched the corners of his mouth. "But, no, Erica,
you're not going anywhere."

"I—"

"Like that."

It took a moment for her to understand. She glanced down to see the white jeans that were perfectly appropriate. Somehow that was all there was. Her bare breasts were as tense as the rest of her body, her small, dark nipples pointing right at him. But then, her breasts and Kyle's hands had always had this magnetic relationship all their own... You're thinking as clearly as a mentally deranged person, she informed herself crisply. But she had won; she understood that. They *were* going. Somehow she had gained ground, even if it was only an inch of the mile she needed to go.

More than once during those hectic two hours of packing and organizing Kyle started to say something. She didn't give him a chance. She played roadrunner in tennis shoes, chattering as if nothing could possibly be wrong, worrying aloud about every detail. She didn't want him to bring up Morgan, not until she had him alone, in a place where he would have to listen. In the meantime, all she wanted was to keep Kyle off-balance. How could he possibly imagine an unfaithful wife, when a chattering magpie was carting a cat around and handing him tennis shoes?

He gave up trying to talk, and finished the packing and other details with a silent, cold efficiency that would have won praise from a computer. She thought unhappily that she could read his mind. All along they had regarded their mini-vacation as a chance to go to a private place to have time to talk seriously about where they stood with each other. What he believed had happened with Morgan didn't change that. They needed to talk—badly. He no longer cared where.

Neither of them mentioned that Morgan's car and trailer were gone. Erica barely took time to breathe; they had to be packed and on their way by nine-thirty. When Kyle's foot pressed on the accelerator to get them to the airport on time, she felt a strange rush of exhilaration, of relief. She knew he'd wanted to walk away, but he hadn't; it made her believe all over again there was something to fight for. Her heart snatched at that mood and held it until they reached the airport.

A very few minutes later, they were standing in front of the plane. It resembled a shiny white toy in the morning sun, with a dozen shiny dials that would have caught a child's eye.

"You've forgotten?" Kyle questioned. "Just step on the mark on the wing."

The wing dipped as Erica put her weight on it. "I'll bet this thing runs by remote control at a baby airport," she marveled aloud.

For the first time all morning, she saw him give a hint of a smile. "Now don't tell me you're nervous. You've flown in dozens of these."

"Awhile back. I loved carnival rides as a kid, too." She felt a gentle swat on her bottom that pleased her enormously. He was trying, and no matter what his feelings, she knew he wouldn't allow them to affect his concentration while he was at the controls. Kyle had earned his license a long time ago through Morgan's father. Flying freight runs paid good money when he was in school. Afterward, Mr. Shane had been both disappointed and a little angry when Kyle refused to join him, preferring to go into business for himself. Morgan's father had wanted Kyle more than he'd wanted his own son in the business . . . but at the moment all Erica could think of was how long it had been since she'd actually flown in one of these little puddle jumpers. Kyle was stowing sleeping bags, totes, a food box, tent, first-aid kit . . . When he was done, he just looked at her, and there was a second smile. "I think we should have hired a seven-forty-seven."

"Listen here. I expected a lot of praise for packing so light—"

"You did, Erica. You packed lightly for snow, rain,

tropical conditions, illness, health, starvation, plague, snakebite..." He vaulted lightly into the seat beside her. "You even remembered to put on a blouse."

She thought he was giving the little white camisole a lot of status. Nevertheless, she smiled. His door was closing; they *were* going. Kyle started the plane's engine and she could feel a thrill of anticipation in her stomach. He held up the mike to announce his departure to the terminal, and let the engine rev for a moment as he handed her a stick of gum.

"Thank you. By the way, you do remember how to fly one of these?" she asked blandly. "It's been a few years..."

"You *are* nervous."

"I'm not. Really. You know what you're doing," she said easily.

"Fine. Do you want to tell me what the hell you're doing, Erica?"

Somehow they were no longer talking about planes. "Do you really want to know?" she asked absently.

"Yes." The word was short, succinct, and chill.

She took a breath, looking at him painfully. "Shaking inside, Kyle." So much for prepared speeches.

"Erica..." He ran a rough hand through the hair at his neck, all anger and impatience. In that quick silence, she sat frozen, but when he finally turned to her there was a half-smile on his lips. "You can stop shaking."

"All right."

"We're going to have a nice easy flight. Lots to see. Neither of us will worry about anything while we're in the air."

"All right."

He sighed, leaning back. "So buckle up."

She buckled up.

"Put the smile back on. A real one."

The smile hovered, became real when he reached over to kiss her mouth. A minute later, the plane trembled as Kyle forced power to the engine, anticipating takeoff.

Very few minutes after that it was gliding down the runway, then up. She could feel everything, every vibration, every hum, in the little Cessna. It was a sensual feeling, almost as if she had a bird's freedom to fly.

They were both quiet for a time, simply taking in the landscape as Kyle piloted the Cessna toward Wisconsin's generously harbored shore on Lake Michigan. Along the way, the rich-colored earth and forests intrigued Erica. From the air, the small country towns seemed to pop out of nowhere, as if pioneers had just cleared the forests yesterday to make room for them and their fields and buildings. But when Lake Michigan suddenly spread across the whole eastern horizon, she could not hold back an audible gasp of pleasure.

Kyle's hand suddenly covered hers. She just looked at him.

"You like that little pond down there?"

She chuckled. "I've seen smaller." He didn't let her hand go until her fingers relaxed in his. The contact seemed to soothe some of his own taut feelings, because he talked more easily then.

As they flew, hugging the coast, Kyle identified for her the wealth of cargoes in the freighters below—iron and iron ore, copper and steel, cars and automotive products, wheat. Erica found herself leaning forward, trying to hear above the hum of the plane's engine. She had never associated the world of business with the water, yet the congestion below was not unlike a city's hustle and bustle. Fortunes were being carted in every direction, the very basics of modern life: fuel, food, and transportation.

"I read somewhere that the Great Lakes contain sixty-seven trillion gallons of water," Kyle said idly. "Would you like to tell me why that crazy figure stuck in my head all these years?"

"You had a mean fifth-grade geography teacher?"

He grinned. "I did at that. But her scare tactics must have been worth something; I've still got the statistics.

The lakes take up some ninety-five-thousand square miles—God almighty, there's the *Wilfred Sykes.*"

"Pardon?"

Kyle motioned below to a huge ship. "It's the biggest ship ever to travel on fresh water, capacity of more than twenty tons—"

"Come on, Kyle. I don't even see how you can identify what ship it is. I mean, I can see it's huge, but..."

Kyle grinned, and the next thing Erica knew she was thrown forward in her seat as Kyle nose-dived to zoom in closer. *Wilfred Sykes* was printed on the side of the huge ship, and Erica's stomach did a somersault.

"See?" he questioned.

"Yes. Thank you, Kyle. Remind me never to doubt you again," she said dryly.

In another twenty minutes, they were soaring toward Green Bay. "It's original name was Bay of the Stinkers." Kyle tossed the comment to her.

"I beg your pardon."

"Stinkers was the French name for the Winnebago Indians," he explained.

She lifted her eyebrows. It was difficult if not impossible to view the scene below as ever having been unsettled. Fisheries, limestone quarries, shipyards, paper mills...and right next to the massive paper factory was a harbor in which floated piles of wooden planks that looked like toothpicks.

The landscape changed rapidly as they headed farther north. First there was Marinette and Menominee, small shipping harbors northwest of Green Bay, and then Escanaba, Michigan, on the northern shore of the lake. Then...

Wilderness. It was as if they were going back in time. Forests stretched as far as her eye could see, dense spruce and balsam. There was an atmosphere of sudden quiet, as if their small aircraft were the only intruding sound.

Kyle had teased her about the black bears around Newberry, but now she could picture them. Bear and moose, beaver and mink, living just as they must have for centuries, totally unaware that civilization threatened the rest of their species. Endless streams and lakes curled into the wild country, sparkling in the sunlight beneath them. For short periods, they couldn't see a stretch of road, not a sign of human life.

It was wild, raw country. The look of it unconsciously evoked a shiver in Erica, half an uncomplicated anticipation at seeing and experiencing something completely new, and half an unconscious awareness of the beauty around her. She was not a pioneer woman and had hardly been raised as one. It was not a place she would want to visit alone, even if the adventuresome spirit struck her.

She raised her eyes to Kyle and studied him. The thought was immediate; there was no place she would hesitate to go with him. Morgan's face flashed in her mind, and when she put aside the memory of his assault, when she tried to remember the best qualities in Morgan and the best qualities she'd thought existed in their friendship, she wondered swiftly why she never *had* been tempted. He had everything she had grown up to value: money, charm, personality, an extravagant lifestyle, and all-American good looks. Other women strayed. Other women with apparently very good marriages seemed to stray . . .

It all seemed so simple, looking at Kyle. She liked his eyebrows; she liked his stride; she liked his knees. During that one hurricane they'd weathered in Florida a long time ago, he'd become exasperated with her when he couldn't get her to move quickly. She'd found it extremely difficult to get alarmed. She'd known he would always put her first; it was difficult to feel fear, knowing that. He was protective and strong and—a little—bull-headed. She loved all of that. Integrity, honesty . . . all those little things that made up such enormous love, right down to what a bear he was when he had a cold. A total bastard when he was ill, really. She loved that, too . . .

Kyle, as if suddenly aware she was staring at him, turned to her and raised one eyebrow. "What on earth are you thinking about?"

"That I don't give a simple damn what you saw. It wasn't like that."

"Pardon?" He couldn't hear her over the engine's hum.

She raised her voice obediently. "I asked you how long before we touch down?"

"Oh . . . another fifteen or twenty minutes."

Erica pushed down the armrest, cupped her elbow on it, and cradled her chin in her palm, waiting. Not long after that, Kyle radioed the tower at Newberry. A flutter of anticipation, and a little fear, settled in her stomach. He was going to have to listen to her. Isolated and totally alone with each other, they were going to have to find a way to talk again—about the things that counted—not Morgan, not their business, not money, not the move to Wisconsin. It seemed to Erica that the wilderness was a perfect place for both of them. Back to nature, back to basics. Back to the thing that mattered at core: the elusive nature of the love they both brought to their relationship . . . or didn't bring.

Ground loomed up to meet the small plane; Erica had the peculiar sensation of falling. Five minutes later, Kyle cut the plane's engine, though for seconds after that she could still hear its incessant hum vibrating in her ears.

"We're here," Kyle said shortly.

13

THE CANVAS TOP of the jeep was a buffeting soundmaker in the wind, and the countryside around them was getting wilder all the time. In Newberry, there had at least been token traffic; for ages now even one passing car was a rarity. Erica unfolded a map and studied it in the last of the late afternoon sun, making a marginal effort to play navigator, though Kyle didn't really need one.

It had taken time to arrange for the plane, pick up the Jeep, and organize their supplies. Then they had stopped to have a snack and buy a few food staples to take with them. Through all of that, they'd both maintained an even mood, yet Kyle had barely spoken for miles now, and was driving north toward Lake Superior as if the devil were after him, on roads not built for speed.

There were more deer-crossing signs than road markers. The endless spruce and balsam and birch forests seemed to encroach more and more on the narrow road, making Erica uneasy; increasingly, it seemed as if they were going nowhere, as if the primitive woods could swallow them in the darkness, and no one would know.

It should have been an opportune moment to talk to Kyle, to explain what had really happened between her and Morgan, and yet she didn't. She was afraid to. His expression was increasingly grim, his whole body tense with concentration, his silence ominous; and the tension kept growing. The gray dusk finally settled into darkness; wearily, Erica leaned back. Vermillion could not be far now. Finally, she dozed off.

She awoke to the tang of lake air and the crispness of pines, vaguely aware she was in the Jeep, curled up against the door. A soft sweat shirt was draped over her shoulders, nestled under her chin; beneath it she felt kitten-snug, perfectly content. The softest click next to her ear made her stir, unwillingly. Suddenly, her head was falling and collided with a warm, solid cushion...a cushion that chuckled.

"Kyle," she murmured sheepily.

"Don't wake up," he whispered. "Everything's fine, Erica..." He scooped her up and cuddled her close; sleepily she nuzzled her cheek to his chest. He smelled like warmth and freshness, like dreams. "Sleep," he murmured next to her ear. His lips touched her forehead, reinforcing that soothing order.

She was willing. She felt the world falling away, her head against something soft and downy and cool and not nearly as comfortable as Kyle's shoulder. Vaguely, she protested, and felt his finger touch her lips, hushing her again. She loved the feel of that finger. Her lower lip felt like a flower that only opened when touched; she savored that sensation until she felt his hands brush at her waist, where her camisole was tucked in. His knuckles pressed lightly into her stomach as he unsnapped the white jeans soundlessly. She smiled in sleep.

He wanted to make love.

She wanted to make love. She could smell the lake and the trees. She could feel the night all around them like something tangible, privacy and darkness and silence. The rich scent of the man only added to that, a primal, evocative scent that she could inhale, that filled her lungs.

He was leaning over her, his hands parting her jeans. His hands slipped inside the fabric, almost but not quite touching... She murmured at his teasing. As he shifted her just a little, one of his hands slipped to her back, sliding the jeans over the curves of her hips, then down over her thighs, over her calves, then off.

The cool night air was enough to make her shiver—she reached instinctively for him—but not quite enough to make her open her eyes. She was loving the sensations coursing through her too much to open her eyes; in the darkness every nerve ending, every heartbeat, every tactile sense was intensified. Desire was a soft, silky cloud covering all of her, protective and luxurious and sweetly wild.

Her hand brushed his thigh, then moved up to where his legs parted, vaguely aware that for some reason her own legs were no longer cold, but covered by the fabric of a sleeping bag she didn't want. She wanted freedom to twist her legs around him, to scissor him close. He wanted the same. She could feel his arousal in her hand, through his jeans; she could hear his sucked-in breath in that night silence.

She opened her eyes.

Their gaze met that instant in the darkness. Brooding and indigo-dark, his eyes were filled with desire, as deep as the night. She could see a pearl of moisture on his forehead. Two pearls. A row of them. Abruptly, he moved her hand, tucked it into the sleeping bag and zipped the fabric up around her.

"Kyle—"

"Dammit. Sleep, Erica."

She heard him rustling next to her. While she'd been dozing in the Jeep, he'd been busy. He had spread a tarp beneath both their sleeping bags to ward off the night's dampness; their totes were next to both of them. She heard him take off his jeans and slide into the sleeping bag not two feet away from her. He turned on his side, facing away; by that time her eyes had adjusted to the starlight.

Her whole body ached, trying to cope with rejection. In nine years of marriage, she knew his body as well as her own. He had wanted her. His body was stiff with tension from wanting her now; he wasn't sleeping. She knew Morgan was the problem; and she still wasn't sure how to bridge the distance between them. It mattered too much that Kyle believe her. "Kyle..."

His tone was abrupt, as if he'd been waiting for her to try. "We're here to talk, Erica. Not make love."

She took a shaky breath. "You can't think I would let anyone else touch me, Kyle. Not intimately. I know you don't believe that. Please let me tell you what happened—"

"There's no need to," he said harshly. "I *know*, Erica. Now leave it and we'll talk in the morning."

For a long time, she stared up at the sky. Separating was what he wanted to talk about in the morning; she understood that. Believing she'd been with Morgan had only intensified the feelings she'd been afraid he'd had all along. He was angry and he was proud and he'd built an impenetrable wall between them... and she thought of the sweat shirt that he must have dug out solely to make sure she was warm, of the possessive way he had cradled her to him, of his light kiss on her forehead as he'd carried her to the sleeping bag.

No, Kyle, she thought. I just don't understand, I'll admit that, but you're going to have to work harder than you know even to bring up the subject of separating.

She awoke to a watery sunlight on her face and the screeching calls of gulls. Totally disoriented, she sat up immediately... to see the most desolate stretch of beach she had ever seen in her life, strewn with driftwood and fallen logs. Behind her, tall birch and spruce encroached almost to the water's edge. Birds were screaming as they fished for their breakfast, and there was water as far as the eye could see ahead of her, beginning with a splashing, foamy little surf, the lake smoothing to glass beyond.

Rationally, she knew they had reached Vermillion last night, but the fact didn't register until she looked east. The lighthouse, a hundred yards away, was a crumbling structure, all but covered with sand as if it had been deserted for centuries. There was no sign that any human being had been here in years. The silence was eerie, ghostly. Perhaps too many ships' captains had tried to save themselves by following the lighthouse beacon. The air around the whispering sand had a give-up sort of sadness, the isolation complete.

Erica turned quickly to the sound of copper pot meeting copper cup. Kyle's sleeping bag was next to her, but empty. The Jeep was farther down the beach, and the sounds came from the other side of it, along with a wisp of smoke that said Kyle was up and fixing breakfast and had probably built a driftwood fire.

She crouched in the sand and brought out clothes quickly from her tote, suddenly half-smiling—at herself. Her first need was a bathroom, the lack of which startled more than appalled her. Spoiled, Erica . . . There might not be any marble taps or makeup mirrors, but a few thousand acres of privacy lay in the woods beyond the beach.

She headed for the trees. Fallen pine needles, softened with weather and brushed with sand, made a carpet for her bare feet. Inside the woods, it was instantly cool. The breeze from the lake was incredibly crisp; on the beach she had been conscious only of the steady beating of the sun.

She stripped completely and put on fresh jeans and a short-sleeved lime-colored top, leaving her feet bare as she started, with toothbrush in hand, for the shore again. Marital crisis notwithstanding, one did not begin a day without brushing one's teeth . . .

She yelped when her bare toes tested the water. The

playful surf was like ice just melted, and the stones that made up the shoreline were smooth and slippery. She rolled up the cuffs of her jeans and bent down; the splash of ice water on her face destroyed any further illusions of sleepiness. After she had brushed her teeth, she stood up again.

Kyle was standing a few feet from her, his hands on his jeaned hips and his open-necked shirt flapping in the breeze. She liked the way he stood with shoulders back in this desolate country, the sunlight behind him. She saw a man with a bearing of fierce pride, yet those shoulders relaxed just perceptibly as he came toward her, as he took in the tumbling red-gold hair and the rolled-up jeans, the peach freshness on her skin from the icy water, her face tilted up to his.

The kiss wouldn't have happened if she hadn't forced it. She ignored his sudden stiffening and simply reached up; her lips tentatively brushed against his just long enough to feel the slightest answering pressure, the slightest tightening of his hand on her shoulder. He might not want to talk, but he was not immune to her. She rocked back on her heels, smiling at him. "I was worried."

"You didn't sleep well?"

"I slept perfectly well. It was the toothpaste. Whether it was biodegradable. This is a very special place, Kyle, and when we leave it, I don't want to think we've mucked it up in any way."

"I really don't think you have to worry about a dab of toothpaste in sixty-seven trillion gallons of water, love."

The last word had slipped out; she could tell from his eyes. But then, maybe he wasn't quite prepared for her particular brand of nonsense this early in the morning; nor did she make it easy for him to rebuff her when she laced an arm around his waist, hugging him. "I love it. You couldn't have chosen a better place to get away from it all in a thousand years."

"I . . ." He hesitated. "All I could think of a few weeks ago was that I wanted you to see it. I hate to admit that

I didn't think much beyond that, the rough setting and no johns... You aren't used to such accommodations. We could stay in a motel—"

"*You* can. *I* won't. Although if you're not prepared to whittle me a canoe in the next few hours, I might just have to check out the neighboring territory for boats. How can we catch our supper without a boat? And don't tell me we came to a place like this to eat in restaurants in the evenings."

She'd clearly taken him back another five yards, and she felt a rush of satisfaction as intoxicating as champagne. If he wanted a pampered little brat, he'd have to carry around a picture of her when she was a child. It was one of those issues she'd wanted to make clear a very long time ago... She scampered ahead of him, calling back, "But for now, if you've eaten all the food I packed in that box for breakfast—"

"Erica?"

She turned, brushing the burnished hair from her face in the breeze.

"You really like it here?"

"It's lonely and desolate—and one of the most beautiful places I've ever seen."

He strode up behind her, hooking his arm around her neck. "In that case, I might just feed you," he said gruffly.

She laughed when she saw his organized feast. Bananas and nuts and apples, bits of dried pineapple for a sweet tooth. He had set the small metal grill over a small driftwood fire; on that the coffee pot rested, giving off its aroma as she sat down on a log. Kyle kept pushing tidbits at her until she was more than stuffed. Gradually, she watched her husband relax, begin to tease her as he always had... Had Morgan really been their guest for only two weeks? Because even as she absorbed Kyle's good-morning mood, she was suddenly aware of how quiet he had been for those two weeks, how much Morgan had affected Kyle as well as herself.

"You haven't said what you thought of it."

"The lake?"

"Of course the lake, bright one. Superior's the biggest body of fresh water in the world, you know. In the winter, the waters can freeze up to forty feet down, a respectable-sized iceberg."

"Safe skating," she said gravely. "Now tell me something good. You know statistics go in one ear and out the other."

"Hollow between your ears," he said sadly, and she kicked a footful of sand at his ankles. "Let's see... Superior has a tide, just like an ocean. It has also had tidal waves."

"You can only fool some of the people some of the time." She leaned back against the log with her second cup of coffee in her hands.

"Real tidal waves," he insisted, as he looked over the shoreline. "A while ago down in Chicago, Lake Michigan surged up and over the banks so far they had to stop traffic—"

"You're kidding," she said disbelievingly.

"And then there was the *Carl Bradley*. A limestone carrier, a good six hundred feet long, carrying a full cargo near Gull Island. It not only sank, it was broken completely in two. The captain lived," Kyle said musingly. "He said it was a tidal wave that broke his ship apart. Waves up to sixty feet high..."

Involuntarily, Erica shivered. The image was suddenly there in her mind, of the storm and the people caught in it, helpless. It seemed so much a part of this bleak, haunted beach with its lighthouse trying to save people's lives. The waters were right in front of her eyes—so brilliant, dancing in the sunlight. It was an absolutely perfect summer day with the sky of aquamarine and the sands spangled with an almost iridescent brightness... It seemed impossible that the lake had so much potential for betrayal, for treachery and tragedy.

"Tell me about that summer you went treasure hunting," she said suddenly. "How you found this place.

What you were looking for. What ever gave you the idea there was treasure here?"

"History," he answered her last question, as he got up to start putting away the breakfast things. "Six thousand ships were wrecked on the Great Lakes in one twenty-year period. Of course, most of them have been salvaged, but not all. Four ships in particular were lost right off these waters at Vermillion and never found. The *Kamloops* was the biggest, with five hundred thousand dollars' worth of cargo, never recovered. Generally a finders-keepers law applies to sunken treasure, and anyone can discover it after others have tried to salvage and failed."

"So you researched it first?" she asked curiously.

Kyle nodded, starting to douse the small fire with sand. "It was fun, exciting, and the search yielded absolutely nothing. At the time, Morgan's father had promised me a job, and I figured I could afford three weeks off, even with the cost of school. At nineteen..." Kyle hesitated, then turned to stare at her. "At nineteen, all I wanted was to get rich quick. At any cost."

"And you've judged yourself harshly for that ever since," she said swiftly, and stood up, too. Before he could say anything else, she snatched up the nearly empty coffee pot and carted it down to the water. He followed her with the two cups, which was unfortunate. Because when he was right next to her again, she couldn't keep her mouth closed. She stood straight up once more, with the coffee pot in her hand. "You didn't desert your father, Kyle. And you were never responsible for his being unhappy."

"Look. Erica—"

She smiled, ignoring the forbidding look in his eyes. "Let's go see the lighthouse."

"No."

"Why not?"

He took a breath. "Because I want you to see it from the top at sunset." He threw an arm around her shoulders, and they carted their few dishes back to the makeshift

fire. He pressed his lips hard against the her temples,
swift and rough. "Shut up, Erica. Leave it all. Let's just
have a good day."

She couldn't imagine why or how that happened, but
it did. That Kyle went out of his way not to touch her
should have dampened those hours... Well, it did. So
did knowing they were both skirting every issue that was
important to them, like children avoiding facing up to a
problem. What they had to laugh about, Erica had no
idea. But they did laugh.

They were together and alone without responsibilities
for an entire day, a combination that proved irresistible;
Erica had always found the simplest pleasure in just being
with him, and Kyle's only wish seemed to be for her to
enjoy herself. He drove the short distance to Tahquamenon Falls, showing her Hiawatha country as he'd
promised. Tumbling waterfalls cascaded from sheer rock
cliffs, nestled in virgin forest, all lush green and fragrant
with summer scents.

One could rent a rowboat there, to paddle around the
half-dozen falls. Erica told Kyle she was a qualified
oarswoman, and when he took her at her word, they
nearly cascaded over one of the falls. As it was, he ended
up paddling furiously against white water while people
screamed at them from the shore. Drenched and laughing
they finally returned to Vermillion.

Tamer sports seemed a better idea; the day had turned
sultry. Fishing from the shore? It seemed reasonable
enough. Fishing poles weren't all that hard to rig up, but
the only bait seemed to be worms they dug from the floor
of the woods. Erica tried to bait the hook. She didn't
mind spiders and bees, but worms just weren't her cup
of tea.

The fishing wasn't particularly successful. Having
started at the warmest, most somnolent time in the sunny
afternoon, it seemed more natural for them to rest on the
sand with one hand balancing the pole. There *were* fish

out there. They liked the worms. The napping fishermen just failed to reel them in.

They didn't seem to be concentrating too hard on living off the land, and the next problem they faced was starvation. Granola bars and raisins went only so far. Laziness had become infectious, and neither one of them really wanted to leave this private little wilderness; they had to bully each other into preparing a meal. They grilled hamburger over an open fire as the sun went down, then toasted marshmallows, which they ate as they sipped their wine. Both had cast-iron stomachs. A blessing.

By the time dinner was over, their laughter was muted with tiredness. They were both content to lie down on their sleeping bags, watching the fire die down, watching the stars take on added brilliance. A crescent moon hung low and lazy, and the steady lap of the lake against the shore created a hypnotic rhythm of private promises.

It was so natural for her to want to touch him. The night belonged to the senses, and the day had been full of pleasures. Instinctively, Erica's hand reached out to touch Kyle's. Just as instinctively, his larger hand curved around hers, his thumb gently stroking her wrist. For a moment, it was fine. Closing her eyes, she could feel the warm current flow between them. It changed only gradually to something warmer, more restless, like a slow rush of flame where their fingers touched. Kyle's hand tightened in hers.

Just as fast as the flame had taken hold, it was extinguished. He jerked up suddenly, leaning forward, staring at the black waters of the lake lapping so gently on the shore.

She stared at the slope of his back for only a second before he spoke. "I think I'll walk for a while, Erica."

Without you. No, sweetheart, she thought. We're not going to end another day with both of us unable to sleep. "I'm tired, but not quite tired enough to sleep. Have one more glass of wine with me before you go?"

He conceded to that. She poured his wine, a nice full Styrofoam cupful. She leaned back as he did, careful not to touch him. A shooting star cascaded down into the depths of the lake, lost like a single spark of fireworks. The whole beach had turned golden by starlight, dark treasures of shadows and hollows in the sand. Kyle's eyes were shuttered at half-mast, not closed.

He didn't want to go for a walk. He didn't want to risk touching her, she thought idly, feeling like a general fighting a war without troops. The loneliness frightened her. Maybe it was Morgan. But maybe it was just that Kyle really didn't want to get close again. Ever.

She was willing to fight, but it was so . . . hard. Kyle didn't move when she stirred a few feet from him, to unroll the sleeping bag she'd been using as a pillow.

"Sleepy now?" he murmured.

"Very."

She'd never been less sleepy in her entire life.

14

ERICA TOOK A slow walk into the woods and stood in the pitch-black shadows of the trees. He couldn't see her; she knew that, and she took a long time, pulling off her shirt and jeans, then slowly removing her panties and bra. A thousand things were in her mind, a restless kaleidoscope of uncertainties.

She'd taken too long to tell him about Morgan; now she didn't know how.

No, that wasn't true. The problem was that she'd never known how. To tell him the truth was one thing. For him to believe her was another. For months now, he'd seemed to lack trust, faith in her. At home...

But they weren't at home now. There, all she could think of was convincing Kyle of the truth about Morgan; here on this wild, deserted beach, she knew Morgan wasn't the point. What she had to tell Kyle; what she wanted to tell him; what she needed him to believe... was that she loved him.

And she desperately wanted to hear that back from him.

"Erica? You're all right?"

Her head jerked up at the sound of Kyle's voice. He had lurched to a sitting position and was staring in her direction. Even by moonlight, she could see the frown etched on his forehead. She was taking a very long time preparing for sleep.

"Fine," she called back.

She lifted her head, closing her eyes. The virgin woods, the total darkness, the primitive rustlings of animals in the brush—all echoed her own restlessness, her own impatience. Thinking accomplished nothing. Not here. Survival was a matter of the senses here, of feel and hearing and scent. Of instincts.

She stepped out of the cover of darkness. Moon rays shimmered over her skin as her toes dug into the soft, cool sand. A whispering breeze from the lake lifted her hair, teased her breasts. It was a warm breeze. Ahead of her the lake seemed untouched by that wind, smooth and black and fathomless. Cool. She'd never in her life walked naked outdoors at night. The warm wind on her bare flesh touched another primitive instinct, as though there were a soft voice deep inside of her, promoting woman and night, urging her to follow her natural, sensual instincts. She could have sworn the lake was calling her . . .

Her toes touched the first of the smooth, slippery stones at the edge of the lake, and she winced at the icy chill of the water.

"Erica?"

"Not to worry. I just want to cool off before sleeping," she called back.

He said something else; she didn't hear it. In four steps, she was up to her knees; at the sixth step, she dived cleanly into that shocking ice bath and surged up again. Every nerve ending burst into life. She whipped back her rope of wet hair and dived again.

The water was both torture and pleasure, a curious combination. The lake was so totally black and endless that she felt a shiver of fear, yet that icy silk embraced her body, seeming to flow in, around, and all through her, intimate and possessive.

She couldn't have explained in a thousand years why she'd gone into the water; it was instinct more than logic. Her arms sliced through the black water in soundless strokes. Then her slow crawl gradually picked up pace. More instinct. She felt wild, frightened, free. Her heart kept drumming out those rhythms of feeling. Her stroke drove her farther, as if she could swim forever, as if she would never tire, as if she could span oceans.

She couldn't. It hit her all at once that the chill water had finally seeped into her bloodstream. Her limbs were tiring, and her lungs were desperately hauling in air. Suddenly, she could see nothing but black sky and water. The shore could not really be so far, yet she couldn't see it in the darkness. Panic hovered over her. She rolled onto her back and simply tried to breathe, to tell herself that her arms weren't too tired to tread water. All she had to do was relax . . .

A sure, firm hand curled at the nape of her neck, and she opened frightened eyes.

"Easy, honey." Kyle's face was white by moonlight; his hair a sleek, shiny black helmet. Water was streaming down his neck, glistening on the deeply etched lines of his forehead. His grim, taut expression was a total denial of the voice dipped in velvet, gentle and soothing. "You're all right?"

Undoubtedly, she would have found her second wind; she had no cramp; she would probably have made it back to shore with flying colors. Those were thoughts, not instincts. She was terrified. "No," she whispered.

She didn't have to say anything else, and Kyle didn't waste words. He turned on his back, drawing her on top of him. His legs and arms treaded water, but his chest was ballast, safe haven. She lay back, just breathing in and out until the long, gulping breaths calmed.

After a time, he shifted upright, bracing her arms on his shoulders. "You're cold as hell, love. We're almost in. Can you sidestroke next to me?"

She nodded weakly. "It was just suddenly so . . . dark.
I got so frightened. Stupid of me, Kyle . . ."

"Everything's fine." His voice was so sure, so calm,
so soothing. "Just go easy, Erica. I'll be right next to
you. So close you can touch me; you can reach out and
hold on any time you want to. Come on, love."

He let her go, hovering as she forced her arms to
scissor through the water. He sidestroked next to her.
Every time she opened her eyes she could see his, watching her, dark and soft, within touching range. All those
primitive instincts surfaced again, a wealth of feeling
that washed through her physical exhaustion. He had
come. Safe haven was within touching range; the love
was there, the strength and power of feeling were there.
He'd had to know before she had herself that she'd over-
estimated her physical strength. He'd had to plunge into
the water before the thought had even crossed her mind
that she was in trouble.

And now she heard his murmured encouragements
next to her, coaxing her to make those last few strokes
until her feet could touch bottom. Her hands pushed
through the water those last few times, finding a strength
she could have sworn she didn't have.

At last her toes touched the lake bottom, and she
surged up to a standing position, breathing in heavy,
gasping pants. Kyle's arms went around her, and her
fingers dug into his back, desperate for him to stay close,
not leave her. In, out; in, out. *Air.* Her arms and legs
ached; her stomach ached; her shoulders ached; *everything* ached.

Kyle's hand brushed back her damp hair, whispering
something she didn't hear. It didn't matter. He cradled
her close, and where her skin touched his she was no
longer cold. Her bare breasts were crushed hard against
his chest, so hard that they hurt, but it was her own hold
forcing that locked-in position. The chill water kept lap-

ping at her hips. Warmer night air brushed the tears from her tired eyes.

Finally, he whispered, "All right now?"

"All right," she agreed, meaning it.

That soothing, sure voice disappeared. He held her away from him, his wet hands on her bare shoulders, and she stared up in shock at eyes suddenly turned absolutely furious. "What the *hell* did you think you were doing?"

"What?"

"Dammit, you could have gotten a cramp! Since when are you an Olympic swimmer, Erica? Going out that far—I could shake you!"

He was rigid with anger, a rage she'd never guessed at. His touch and tone had been gentle, so sure, so soothing in the water, without even a hint of any other emotion. She'd never been physically afraid of Kyle in their nine years of marriage, couldn't even conceive of it, but she knew at that moment he was very close to doing just what he'd said—shaking her. Because he was terrified of what might have happened to her. Instincts, she thought happily. She'd never trust another rational thought as long as she lived.

"*Answer me!* And if you ever do a damn fool thing like that again—"

She raised herself up on tiptoe, fitting her lips to his. His mouth clamped down on hers so hard she would have fallen, except that her body was drawn up, tugged into intimate contact with his. On a dry, hot day, tinder ignited just that easily. Lake Superior . . . that single largest body of fresh water in the world . . . His hands rushed over her as if he could warm her shivering body in spite of all those gallons of ice water. He could. Without much effort.

She was shuddering with chill . . . yet she wasn't, suddenly. Fire warmed her veins, a fierce, wild, primitive fire . . . She wrenched her mouth from his only for a mo-

ment. "You love me, Kyle. Don't try to tell me you
don't," she whispered.

"Dammit. You know I love you. And I swear if you
ever do anything like that again—"

He would murder her. Fine. She savored the thought.
For someone who'd been afraid of anger all her life, she
suddenly relished his, understanding it was a measure of
how much he loved her. More instincts, she thought
fleetingly. She didn't need words; she'd been listening
to words for months, had torn herself apart with words.
From now on, she would listen only to her different heart.

He grabbed her hand and pulled her toward the shore,
stopping only when they'd reached the pebble-strewn
sand. "Wait here," he barked. She couldn't imagine where
he thought she would go.

He stalked back from the campsite seconds later with
a cotton blanket that he drapped over her, rubbing her
thoroughly until her flesh came alive again and took on
heat. She couldn't seem to stop looking at him. His
hands, so fiercely rubbing her skin, were trembling. Chill
water was still streaming down his body; he didn't seem
to notice.

His bold features were forbiddingly carved, but that
wasn't the message his eyes were sending her. His eyes
were dark blue and full of torment, registering that she
was safe, measuring the loss he had nearly suffered.

It was no small effort for her to extricate herself from
the blanket he had so possessively swathed her in. She
managed, taking him off-guard as he was about to begin
scolding her again. All she had to do was brush her hands
over the taut muscles of his shoulders, and the next thing
she knew he had snatched her up tight against his chest,
his head buried in her hair and the blanket lying forgotten
in the sand.

"God, Erica, if anything had happened to you . . ."

"Hold me," she whispered. "Keep on holding me . . ."

Kyle's body was cool and damp; it was her turn to

do the warming. She didn't bother with a blanket. Although she had been freezing just short minutes before, she had never felt warmer than now, had never felt more capable of wrapping him up in the warmth that emanated from her soul. Her hands swept over his shoulder and his long, lean back. Her breasts, warm and full, absorbed his chill; her bare thighs pressed his. The friction of her lips rubbing against his was so frenzied that it could have started a fire.

Kyle slowed his pace. His whole body shuddered, but no longer from chill. Gently, his palms cradled her head, framing her face, his thumbs tracing the satiny texture of her cheeks as if he would memorize the shape and feel of her features. When he let his hands fall, it was only to wrap his arms around her again, this time with tenderness, and his lips pressed kiss after kiss in her hair.

She inhaled, feeling a love so strong it hurt, a love so strong she felt a crazy blur of tears in her eyes that blurred the landscape around her, doubled the stars, added silver to the sand, enriched the dark shadows with an ebony sheen.

"How I love you," she whispered. "How I love you, Kyle. Only you. There was never anyone else." The words spilled out in a desperate rush. "There was never Morgan. No matter what you think happened, no matter what he told you—"

"Erica. Don't lie." He wrenched her hands from him and stepped back, his face suddenly a dark, expressionless mask. "I never needed Morgan to tell me what happened. I knew. And the hell of it was that I understood." Without another word, he turned his back on her and stalked up the sandy shore toward their camp.

Erica stared at Kyle's retreating figure for all of a minute before chasing after him. Furiously, her hand closed on his upper arm, catching him off-balance and forcing him to face her. "What exactly is it that you think you know?" she demanded.

"Stop it."

She shook her head wildly. "No way, Kyle. You've *got* to listen to me."

He sighed, throwing back his head, resting his hands on his hips. "I understand," he said bitterly. "I've understood from the first. I'm not judging you, Erica. I've been in your shoes."

"You stop it. *Stop* talking in riddles, for godsake, Kyle. You've been trying to tell me something for months. Just *tell* me!"

"Look," he said harshly. "There's nothing to tell. I could *see*. History repeating itself." He took a breath. "When I was a kid, we had only a cookstove for heat in the winter, Erica. People looked down on the McCrerys; walking to school in tennis shoes through the snow. My father just didn't give a damn about anything from the time my mother died. No one could have accused me of lack of loyalty toward him; I loved the man. Really loved him, as a child. But as I grew older, the anger and resentment kept building, at things we could have had that we never did, at security that was never there . . . I declared my love and loyalty so loud and strong that I didn't know what they'd really turned into, until it was too late.

"You think I was going to stand around and watch your love turn into resentment, Erica? You declared your loyalty with never a single resentful word, as if you had a little halo around your head. You're never going to tell me that you didn't have second thoughts about our moving to Wisconsin, that you didn't resent the changes in our lifestyle. How I could see myself in you! I never showed an ounce of resentment toward my father, either—and maybe that's why I never saw what was happening between us until it was too late. And no, it wasn't a damned cookstove, Erica, but I brought you down—"

If she were a man, she would have shaken him. As it was, her eyes blazed up at his, filled with hurt and pain. "You didn't bring me down, you stubborn bastard! *When* are you going to get that through your head? The only time you hurt me was when you failed to share your feelings with me. I had a *right* to know what you were feeling. I had a *right* to know you were mucking up everything in your head—"

In spite of the pinched look in his eyes, he allowed himself a twist of a smile at her choice of words. "Erica. You had a right to your choices. You had a right to say what you needed and wanted. The ring on your finger— I couldn't turn it into a prison chain. That wouldn't have been love—and I'd *been* chained by ties that destroyed love. I was locked in by the debts I owed to my father— financial, moral . . . Hell, you know I love the wood. I've been trying to tell you that you're no prisoner, Erica. I've been trying to tell *myself* that loving you meant ensuring that you had choices."

Her whole body suddenly went still in shock, even before the import of what he'd said registered in her head. "Are you trying to tell me that you *knew* Morgan was coming on to me? You *knew?*"

His body had turned to stone at the tone of her voice; his eyes were searching hers, but he was silent. "You *knew?*" She kicked a footful of sand at him. Then leaned down and picked up a fistful of it, hurling at him. The sand connected with his chest, and she reached down to pick up another handful. He dodged the spewing sand that would have connected with his face; his eyes were suddenly blazing like her own. She couldn't have cared less.

"Was that the idea? Letting me experience someone else's love so that I could make a *choice?*"

"*NO!*"

The word came from his gut, but she was no longer listening. She whirled around in a tempest of red-gold hair and started running. Her toes dug into the sand so hard they hurt; air clogged so tight in her lungs that it choked her. When he'd said he understood about Morgan, she thought he meant that Morgan had talked to him first, told him lies. She never dreamed that Kyle had known that Morgan was coming on to her like a heavy-handed octopus and never lifted a finger to help her . . . *Love?* A few minutes ago, every instinct had told her she had his love. Now the pain kept coming, like needle-sharp waves. He *let* that happen? She barely heard his husky voice, rasping with emotion.

"Erica . . ."

"You just leave me completely alone!"

— 15 —

THERE WAS ONLY one place to run to in that deserted landscape.

A jagged concrete arch was all that remained of the door to the lighthouse. The floor was covered with sand, and straggly weeds weaved near the curved steps; moonlight illuminated the eerie entrance. The spiral staircase wound upward. She wanted a haven, and she wanted to be *alone*, and she didn't care that the staircase looked unsafe and very, very old.

The first step held when she put her weight on it, and the second and the third. The fourth creaked ominously, and Erica balanced herself with her hand on the cement wall, her heart beating frantically. Whatever railing might have been there at one time no longer existed. The fifth step seemed to tremble beneath her foot, and her heart stopped beating completely. She went down on hands and knees as a child would.

"Erica, dammit! It isn't safe at night—"

"Leave me alone!"

Finally, she reached the top and took a deep, an-

guished breath. The floor of the lighthouse was solid,
but there was no longer a roof or windows, no longer a
desk or the instruments a lighthouse keeper might have
taken for granted a long time ago. All she could see was
the sky above the lake. The stars glittered above the water
like a spray of diamonds.

It was all there. The place where ships had counted
on the beacon of light to save them. The place where
men would have died if that beacon of light had failed.

She could feel Kyle's presence the moment he reached
the top of the stairs, but she refused to turn around. She
was trying to catch enough breath to fill the emptiness
in her lungs, in her heart.

"You're going to listen."

"The hell I am."

He blocked the stairs, moving directly into her line
of vision. She didn't want to look at him, but his bold
features held her gaze. His strong nose and brilliant blue
eyes, his thick, black hair curling in the wind, his brawny
shoulders and his pride . . . the loneliness of his pride,
she thought achingly. And told herself desperately that
she didn't care.

His voice came out a thick baritone, vibrating with
emotion. "I needed some sign from you, Erica. That it
wasn't just loyalty that kept you by my side. I asked you
for it, in every way I knew how. I always knew Morgan
cared about you, and I always knew you regarded him
as a brother. He could offer you every damned thing that
I no longer could. Everything I'd taken from you by
moving to Wisconsin. I *had* to know it was more than
loyalty that kept you by my side—"

"Kyle—"

"Hush."

Startled, she leaned back against the ragged cement
edge and stared at him.

"So, in principle, I wanted you to test any waters you
needed to test," he said heavily. "The reality was a little

different." He moved toward her, one slow, stalking step at a time. "The reality was seeing you after the belling, guessing what he'd tried to do to you. You never wondered where the hell I was for all those hours later that night? I went crazy, Erica. I did more than send him packing—"

"*You* sent him packing!" Erica sputtered through a furious sparkle of tears. "*I* sent him packing. I told him to take a hike, to leave me alone. To leave *us* alone."

Later she would realize that the bleak, haunted look had left his expression, had disappeared the instant she picked up that fistful of sand and hurled it. All she knew at the moment was that he was a desperately unfair, cruel man. Gently, he reached out to brush away a tear that trembled on her cheek. His palm cradled her face, then smoothed away a single strand of hair that had fallen down over her forehead.

"Dammit. Don't," she said shakily.

"Tell me," Kyle said, his voice vibrant. "Just tell me..."

Never, she thought—but the words burst out as if the dike had been washed away. "I felt so awful," she burst out. "Kyle, he was your friend, and I thought he'd come to help us. To help *you*. I kept trying to believe I was misunderstanding him... I'd hugged Morgan a thousand times! I hug my mother; I've hugged Martha; dammit, I've hugged the cat! I never thought anything about it. I've never felt so guilty in my entire life, suddenly realizing how he must have seen it... I was so damned *stupid*..."

"Oh, my love..."

"And then he threatened to tell you that I'd... that we'd... I was so scared to tell you, that you wouldn't believe me, that you'd believe *him*..."

"I thought you wanted to come here to talk about a separation, Erica. I thought..." His palms cupped her face, raising it so he could look into her eyes. "You told me you'd had enough, if we couldn't go back the way we were. We can't go back to the Florida lifestyle, Erica, the affluence . . ."

She shook her head helplessly. "Kyle, I was talking about love, not money. I thought you didn't love me anymore, that you were trying to push me away. That's why I thought *you* wanted to come here, that you were trying to be kind by taking me away from everyone, so you could tell me—"

"*Never* that," he whispered. He turned her around and pulled her back against him, folding his arms under her breasts, cradling her against his thighs. His chin nuzzled her hair back so that her neck was bare for the soft kiss he placed there. "Never that," he repeated. "All I wanted was to bring you to a place where you couldn't escape. I thought that if we could just *be* together I could remind you how much love we've always had, Erica. No matter how things changed, no matter how I thought your feelings had changed, I still wanted a chance to show you . . . I can give you a wealth of security in terms of *love* . . ."

Her arms covered his, tightening as his did. "Oh, Kyle . . ."

"It took me so damned long to get my own house in order. I wanted so much for you, Erica. The world. I saw too much in terms of *things*, because I wanted the best life for you. I still want the best, the most of laughter and loving, the most of sharing and commitment. I just didn't know what real security was until I thought I'd lost it."

She twisted in his arms, lifting her head up to stare at him, her eyes searching his. "Couldn't you have shared it?" she whispered. "After nine years of marriage, couldn't you have let me know how badly you were hurting, Kyle? Couldn't you have trusted me to understand, instead of keeping all your hurt inside you?"

His mouth dipped down on hers, blocking out the soft moon rays, sweeping her up in that sensual world they'd always shared with each other. She felt his pain, something he had never been able to communicate before, his desperate grappling with his instinctive pride. Now he told her, with exquisite, sensitive tenderness. His fingertips trembled in her hair, combing the strands over and over, winding the silk in his hands. His lips whispered over her forehead, her eyes, her cheeks, His chest rubbed against the tightening tips of her breasts, and his thighs grazed hers.

"I made the sunburst for you," he said softly. "I see you that way, as my sun. As light and fire and softness, sometimes elusive, always warming everyone around you, Erica. Should it be easier because we have nine years behind us? I think it's harder. I love you so much more, with so much more depth; we've shared so much. The thought of losing you now is infinitely more painful even than when I first loved you. I feel so... vulnerable. I feel that in loving you I should always be able to do the best thing for you, even if it hurts me..."

By unspoken agreement, they made their way back down the circular stairs, and walked across the sand to their camp. They bundled their sleeping bags into their arms and retraced their steps to the lighthouse. Erica listened as Kyle kept talking, anticipating much of what he had to say... needed to say out loud. He hadn't turned to her in time of trouble—out of shame. He'd turned his back on his father when he was eighteen to make his own way, at a time when Joel was drinking heavily and needed him. At eighteen, Kyle could take no more of poverty, of insecurity, of responsibilities he'd carried from the time he was a small child.

Financially, he'd continued to care for his father, but the burden of desertion had always weighed heavily on his conscience. He wasn't proud of his actions, and he hadn't wanted Erica, who was raised in health and sunshine and silver-spoon security, to know about the kind of childhood he'd had. But when his father was dying, he had accused Kyle of running out on everything that really mattered to him, not only on his father, but on his love of wood, his roots.

Joel had accused Kyle of running and had challenged him to come home to see if he wasn't right. "And he *was* right," Kyle said quietly. "The need to work with my hands was always there, the urge to create in my own way. The need to make the McCrery name mean something again, as a last loyalty to my dad. And as a loyalty . . . to myself."

They spread the sleeping bags side by side at the top of the lighthouse again and stretched out on their sides, with a star-sprinkled sky for a ceiling, their haven a symbol of shelter in that lonely landscape. Erica listened, the puzzle pieces all falling into place, aching for the man who'd tried so hard to do right, even as a small boy. She could finally see so clearly how he'd confused love with loyalty thinking that the two were in opposition. She reached over to touch his face, to smooth away the last lines on his forehead. He pressed a kiss into her palm.

She wanted desperately to tell him that he had nothing to feel guilty about, that he had been as good to his father as any son could be. In time, perhaps, he would listen to her; she knew he had been working out the feelings all through these many months. Now it seemed more important that she just listen; that was what he most needed from her. And she needed to hear that he was willing to solve those problems through the channel of communication that they'd allowed to develop. It was never Joel McCrery or Morgan who had nearly destroyed their relationship; it was their own failure to talk to each other. Clearly.

Erica was willing to talk all night.

Kyle was willing to talk all night.

Something happened, though, as they continued to speak in whispers. They found other ways of communicating, as she touched his face, as he touched her hand, as they stared at each other so long in the moonlight. The night breeze obliged them by turning cool; they moved closer together. Two sleeping bags were suddenly too many.

Her knee touched his and found itself captured between his long legs. He couldn't seem to keep his hands out of the sun-gold of her hair. Erica, as aware as Kyle of what was happening, smiled radiantly.

She heard a husky growl that sounded suspiciously like laughter at her response, from deep in his throat. She heard it, and then she felt it when his lips teased an evocative little message on hers. "Mrs. McCrery, through thick and thin, you may have noticed that a few things have never changed."

She slid her hand down his side, over his lean ribs to his narrow hips, watching his whole body tense in response. She tried it again, with even more pleasing results. Restlessly, he drew her hips closer to his with one long leg, his hand beginning a gentle, sweet discovery of her left breast, as if he'd never touched it before. "What has never changed?" she inquired lightly.

"Your body loves mine."

"I think your body is the problem, Mr. McCrery. It's got a one-track mind. It always has had." She sucked in her breath when he leaned over her, his tongue replacing his hand on her breast. "Kyle . . ."

"In a minute, Erica."

A minute was just too long. She forgot the thought. There was a time for lovemaking that took hours, and a time for loving that captured all the emotions in short order. This was a short-order time. It was all there, the lonely trial they'd put each other through, their renewed hope and faith in the future, their stronger feelings of love. And the first time they made love that night, it was with a desperate need to deal with all of that, a hunger to reseal the bonds of commitment, a desire born of love, an urgent need to please and know each other. And last, the simplest wish, to communicate with each other on a level beyond words.

Afterward, Kyle held her close, still warming her in his arms, pressing soft, tender kisses on her forehead, in her hair. She lay still, watching the stars above them, feeling precious and cherished and well, well loved. They would survive; she knew that. There would be other crises; she knew that, too. That came with the territory of marriage. The thought filled her with more anticipation than fear. Their love measured up, had strength to endure all trials.

She curled up against his chest, only gradually waking from the aftermath of loving to look up at him. His turquoise eyes deepened to sapphire by starlight; she loved that. "I'm sorry," she said gently, "about Morgan. Sorry you lost a friend."

"He wasn't," Kyle said simply. "I think I've known that for a long time, really. But his family was so good to me when I was in school."

"Loyalty again, Kyle?" she asked.

He kissed her forehead, lightly branding her.

"Where exactly *were* you the night after the belling? I waited and waited—"

"At the hospital."

Her eyes widened in surprise, staring at him in the darkness. "At the—?"

"Morgan broke his nose. He had to be patched up before he could take that trailer of his back where it came from, Erica. I don't understand how he could have fallen against that packing crate—"

"Kyle! You *hit* him?"

"Of course not. Grown men don't hit other grown men. You were the one who sent him away, Erica. That's what counts." He leaned over and kissed her chin, then the small hollow in her throat. "I came damned close," he whispered, "to taking that St. Christopher's medal around his neck and strangling him. You haven't got a perfect husband, Erica. If anyone knows that, you do. He cracked a rib, too. On another packing crate."

"Kyle—"

His lips touched down on her shoulder. "Mine," he whispered. The same lips captured her right breast, neglected until now in favor of the left one. "Mine," he whispered. "I don't like people who hurt you, Erica."

They headed into the takeoff between her third and fourth rib. Ignition, payload, soar. Poor Morgan, she thought fleetingly. A lonely ship in the night that foundered for lack of light. She had her lighthouse, her beacon, to guide her to shore. She had her love.

All Titles are $1.95

Available at your local bookstore or return this form to:

SECOND CHANCE AT LOVE
Book Mailing Service
P.O. Box 690, Rockville Centre, NY 11571

Please send me the titles checked above. I enclose _____ Include 75¢ for postage and handling if one book is ordered; 25¢ per book for two or more not to exceed $1.75. California, Illinois, New York and Tennessee residents please add sales tax.

NAME _____

ADDRESS _____

CITY _____ STATE/ZIP _____

(allow six weeks for delivery)   SK-41b